T0165445

Concealed Existence

Concealed Existence

UNCONCEALED

AKSHAT GUPTA

PARTRIDGE

ISBN: Hardcover   978-1-4828-7454-9
               Softcover   978-1-4828-7453-2
               eBook   978-1-4828-7452-5

Print information available on the last page.

To order additional copies of this book, contact
Partridge India
000 800 10062 62
orders.india@partridgepublishing.com

www.partridgepublishing.com/india

CONTENTS

Special thanks to Mom-Dad,
Bulbul Goyal, Ananta, Avinash, Aradhya,
Ritesh Sharma and Saurabh Mhatre.

1 - UNIDENTIFIED JOURNEY

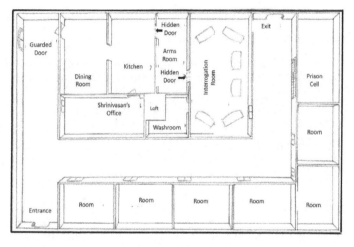

(11.6755 degree North, 92.7626 degree East)Ross Island happens to be the most aesthetic piece of land in the Andaman & Nicobar Islands, about 2km east of Port Blair. It beckons you to take in the serenity of nature's finest gifts with the inheritance of rare, yet significant species. Adorning the island, laid a dome-shaped high-tech facility.

Purely built for the purpose of research on the isolated land, the magnificent empire would awestruck even the most sumptuous of men. Equipped with the latest modern technology, the facility boasted of state of the art coastal and marine monitoring systems. Designed and constructed with only glass, the facility exploited surface technology to its best. Each screen you lay your hands to, would start talking to you as if it was a part of an advanced species, iterating the temperature and atmospheric pressure around you, making life easier in aspects unimagined.

As brilliant as it was in these aspects, it was even more so when it came to security. Motion sensor cameras were installed in each corner of the arched roof. No one was ever alone inside the dome. The digital eye accompanied wherever one went.

Early morning, as soon as Veerbhadra, an ex-Indian army Brigadier, voluntarily retired, left his premise and entered the dome's lobby, he spotted a captive surrounded by four armed guards, handcuffed and blind folded. "He is "The Man"", thought Veerbhadra.

Veerbhadra had to come to this place as the security chief, with the team of 21, including gunmen and guards. He was there on a mission. Being the finest of the men that his cult possessed, he was summoned for various missions, confidential or public, by various organizations throughout the world. This one was different from others.

Veerbhadra was six feet tall. He had lived well the past 40 years of his life, a substantial part of it devoted to the army. His face was that of an average man, not so well-featured. His skin dusky, and the short military cut, salt and pepper hair added to his rough look. Some bruises and scars on both his hands, not very old, imparted the truth of his battles and their intensities. His hard muscular body was evident under his black jeans, white t-shirt, and brown leather jacket. His eyes were masked by black aviator glares. He was always aware of his pistol, well concealed on his waist behind the jacket's fall, no matter what the situation at hand.

Veerbhadra ordered one of the guards to unmask the man. He took off his glares. A scar parallel to his right eye was now in view, and his jet black eyes were set upon the man before him. The man's face would not even once give away the fact that he was nearly half done with his life. At about forty years of age, he appeared pretty young. His face was ethereally carved, his skin so charming and luminous, that he formed an aura of beauty around him. The man had stayed in the dark for quite long, evident from the way he flinched before his eyes got fully accustomed to light. His eyes were intense and deep, a hue of sea blue. They seemed to possess the power of hypnotism. Veerbhadra stood amazed for a moment.

The man looked with astonishment on his face, which was inevitable. Veerbhadra saw that look and half smiled. He remembered well how he had felt when he had stepped into this massive dome for the first time. He was mesmerized, overcome by the mere vastness of the place.

After the man stabilized himself, which took him a couple of seconds, he looked at Veerbhadra, quite aware of the two guns aimed at him.

Veerbhadra and his boss had been waiting for this man, though he didn't precisely know why. All he knew was that the man they were searching for was found and was to be interrogated. About what, he didn't know but was sure that it was something very serious. Veerbhadra was now impatient to know what. He didn't like being half informed. He ought to know the whole story. He deserved to stand in the innermost circle. If not, why was he ummoned at all?

He had worked with the most powerful of men and knew their ways well. But his new high command was strange. He had been anxious of everything, still maintained whatever the big secret he had, as confidential.

The captive was wearing an outdated brown trouser on his belly button line, and a cream shirt with the collar button unbuttoned.

Veerbhadra suddenly found that he was staring at the man in the eye. Something about this man told him that even he held a secret of his own. At the same time he realized that the man was composed to the highest degree. No wave of fear or worry had once crossed his face. Man of courage and confidence.

Approving his thoughts, in an unperturbed tone and gesture, the man offered Veerbhadra a handshake. "Om Shastri", he introduced. Veerbhadra took his hand and replied with a crushing handshake. Contrary to his expectations, Om Shastri didn't wince. Instead, he smiled leaving Veerbhadra still more stupefied.

Apparently, Veerbhadra nearly jumped when his name echoed in a familiar voice in the lobby. It was Dr. Srinivasan, his boss. *"Yes sir"*, he replied. Om Shastri peeped from behind Veerbhadra to look at the man. He could not stop himself from giggling silently.

The man he saw was four feet and eight inches tall, at about 65, and dark skinned like most other South Indians. His lips were dark brownish which revealed that he was a chronic smoker. His white hair covered only the

5

farther part of his scalp. One other aspect that revealed his age was his dowdily dressed appearance. Dr. Srinivasan had donned a brown matte suit, a white shirt beneath, a broad, red, loose tie on his collar. He also wore obsolete black, square framed glasses over his eyes, with a lace that hanged low from the two edges and circumvented his neck.

Dr. Srinivasan's appearance was comical, but his eyes brimmed with discipline. His conduct could command even the top most officials. He was a boss by default. He could give everyone a sense of being a subordinate in his presence. He was funny till he was quiet. It could be easily concluded that he was a no nonsense man and highly dedicated to his work.

Dr. Srinivasan was followed by another fair man. Dr. Batra. He introduced Dr. Batra to Veerbhadra and vice versa. They shook hands warmly. Dr. Batra was a colleague of Dr. Srinivasan, or so it seemed to Veerbhadra.

Veerbhadra took him to be a not so jovial kind of man. He had worn a grumpy look, and was supposedly infuriated. He looked even more educated than Dr. Srinivasan, thought Veerbhadra. His eyes were those of an intellectual.

He was a tall, fair skinned man. Aged 50 years, Dr. Batra belonged to the Sikh community. He had brownish eyes and a chubby face. He wore a maroon formal shirt and black trousers that went along fine with his black leather shoes. Most of the fat that his body had taken in was accumulated around his abdomen. His beard was shaved in style along with his mustaches. He wore a metallic *kadda* (bangle) in his right hand and a classical Roman numeral watch on the left.

Om Shastri had to peep a little farther to catch a clearer glimpse of Dr. Srinivasan. As soon as he did that, his eyes widened and he almost screamed, *"Chinna?"*

All the heads turned towards the sound, astonished.

"What?" asked Dr. Batra in his throaty voice, *"confused"?*

"Nothing", replied Om Shastri.

Dr. Shrinivasan was offended; he felt he was being mocked.

Veerbhadra had never met a man like of Om Shastri. Everything Om did or say, mystified him.

"Is he the one?" asked Dr. Srinivasan in his heavy voice and South Indian accent.

"Aaunu, sir", replied Veerbhadra in Telegu and rectified it immediately *"I mean Yes sir."*

"So whom are we waiting for? Take him to the interrogation room."

The guards, holding their positions around Om Shastri, accompanied him and followed Veerbhadra. They entered an L shaped corridor. Dr. Srinivasan walked straight ahead and Veerbhadra followed him. The passage was sandwiched between plain wall on his left and few doors on his right with a dead end ahead and a sharp left. They came across the edge of the left wall. Two men guarded the only door on his left at the end of the wall and let them in.

Veerbhadra was unaware what was Om Shastri being interrogated for!

The room they entered was about 12 feet high, cocooned in the same posh and ritzy interior as was the dome itself. A chair, crafted out of stainless steel, with a foot rest affixed to it, collateral iron rods serving as the backrest, a black leather seat, and handcuffs integrated into the arm rest happened to be the gist of the room. 'Room' would be unfair to it, Om Shastri mused. It was a laboratory, or so it came across as. Surrounding the chair, were a number of polished wooden tables, initially uncountable to Om Shastri. Each table had a computer screen associated with it.

Ultramodern, concluded Om Shastri. The captive would sit in the center, and the griller would debrief him; dig out answers by hook or by crook. The facility had a projector hanging from the ceiling and a white screen to project on, nailed up on the wall opposite to the projector.

Om Shastri was dragged and pushed to the central seat and tied tight to it by the guards using the already available provisions. His waist, legs, and head were fastened to the chair using leather belts. His eyes and fingers were, as of now, the only movable parts of his body.

All of a sudden, a palm with a piece of cotton covered his nose from behind him. The smell from the cotton was nauseating.

Om Shastri was falling in a plethora of silence.

No thoughts, no feelings, all voices muted...

Meanwhile Veerbhadra was sitting silently observing the cameras. He could sense, not only the captive, but everyone else present in the room was being watched.

It was 11:00 am, Om Shastri opened his eyes, he was still tied to the same chair, in the same place, but the faces around him were none he had seen before. The dull silhouette of each person seated behind the encircling tables was all that he could make out, apart from an intense fog farther away starting from the tip of his nose. He was subconsciously awake.

Om Shastri's rational absence was a consequence of a concentrated narcotic drug that he was compelled to take down his nostrils. His vision blurred because, by trying to arouse himself, he was trying to get into his senses.

All said and done, the interrogation would now commence...

2 - INCONCLUSIVE INCEPTION

The door opened and a lady walked in. She introduced herself as Dr. Shahista to the team. After meeting her colleagues she took over and sat right in front of the captive.

She is a prominent psychiatrist, who was rewarded and applauded for her significant work in the field of hypnotism, and funded for her researches. She was appointed by and for the government as and when needed.

She had been called from Pune, Maharashtra her homeland. She was in her mid-forties. Five and a half feet tall, Dr. Shahista was beautiful, fair complexioned and elegant. She held honor and pride in her personality. However, an aura of optimism surrounded her. Copper brown hair, hung freely past her waist. She never forgot to wear an amiable smile. Apart from that, she wore a black embroidered *kurti,* a half white *patiyala salwaar,* a black printed *dupatta* across her shoulders (one of the Indian traditional dresses), and a pair of traditionally crafted *shoes jootiyaan.*

God had not seen fit to distribute evenly the gift of beauty and brain. But Dr. Shahista possessed both. Cap-a-pie, she was adorned by varying jewel stones worn for all sorts of peace and fulfillment. She carried a *tabeez*(a bracelet kind of ornament to be worn on the biceps) fastened on her left biceps, two golden bangles on the other hand, a thin golden chain round her neck, a few rings with embedded stones affixed on her fingers.

"Who are you?" asked Dr. Shahista to the captive
"Om Shastri", he replied in a state of trance.
"We know that, Mr. Shastri", Dr. Shahista affirmed.
"Tell us what we don't know", she continued.
"You don't know anything", murmured Om Shastri.
"Yes, Mr. Shastri. We don't know things, which is why you are here. But one thing that we know for sure is that this isn't your real name."
"What is your real name?" repeated Dr. Shahista.
"I don't remember", said Om Shastri in his feeble voice.

An unusual answer by a hypnotized person, thought Dr. Shahista.

Sitting on one of the chairs, with a mythological book in his hands, Abhilash said, *"Liar"*.

"He cannot lie", contradicted Dr. Batra, *"he has been injected with the Narco analysis drugs!"* Dr. Batra was clearly frustrated.

"Narco!" said Abhilash as it was French to a greek and continued looking at Dr Batra for a reply.

"It's a truth serum. One cannot lie after it." Concluded Dr Batra in short, showing no interest in its explanation

Dr. Tej Batra, as went his full name, was a sincere and matured person. He was only driven by logic and intelligence. A bit quick tempered, Dr. Batra's behaviour was at times unpredictable. Rare situations uplifted his mood and made him happy.

"And above that, he is hypnotized", intruded Dr. Shahista in firm agreement with Dr. Batra.

Both of them looked at Abhilash, expecting surrender. Abhilash shrugged and whispered, *"There are things beyond medical science."*, and continued reading his book.

Abhilash had spent the 30 years of his life with his head ducked into Hindu mythological books. So his knowledge in the same was unbounded. Being a descendant of a *Brahmin* family of *Raj Purohits* (administrative priests) in a small town called *Ambikapur*, he was treated in his place like Gods powered by superstitious believes and people. Endowed with the highest forms of respect and prestige, he was guarded by the pride in his attitude. Criticizing others for their mistakes was in his blood.

He was a 5 feet and 8 inches tall, dark complexioned man with plum physique. He was wearing an ill fit white *kurta* unaware about his belly popping out, paired with blue denim jeans. Abhilash was a staunch believer of myths and superstitions. His appearance proved it. He had put on various rings with various stones, and for various purposes. Without being asked for one, he never failed to give his advice on what stone to trust in a particular problem. A *raksha sootra* (protective strand made up of cotton), was tied on his left hand's wrist. His neck carried a *rudraksh* (A seed of a plant believed to be a shield against bad luck and ill-health) string. His forehead had a U-shaped *sandalwood tilak* traced on it and he had put on *kolhapuri chappals* (slippers) in his feet. He carried an old-fashioned jute bag on one of his shoulders that contained a few books on Hindu *mantras* (verses).

"Tell us whatever you remember, Mr. Shastri.", Shahista came back to the point.

Om Shastri's face reflected a myriad of expressions smiling, calmed, tensed, afraid and rapidly changing as he spoke.

"I remember Banda Bahadur", Om Shastri uttered with his eyes closed.

"Who is he?", Abhilash demanded.

"My general", said Shastri.

"Is he also a part of your team?"

"Yes."

"Where is he now?"

"He is dead."

"How did he die?"

"He was killed."

"Who killed him?"

"Farkhseer did."

"Whom else can you recall?"

"Sanjay!"

"Who Sanjay? Sanjay Dutt? Sanjay Suri? Or Sanjay Leela Bhansali?" retorted Abhilash in a sarcastic tone.

A girl guffawed. LSD- Lisa Samuel D'costa. A professional hacker, LSD was involved in a lot of online forgery and bank account seizure. At a young age of 25, she had caught the attention of the Indian Cyber Cell. But she was least bothered about that. She had all the expertise without a degree. LSD was a beautiful girl, raw and unpolished in her mannerisms, smart and intelligent in her work. She had an offhand outlook towards everything but her job.

"Could be Sanjay Manjrekar", LSD chuckled.

LSD played it fast and loose. Her tongue was seldom in her power. She had a face anyone could see through to instantly know her random thoughts. LSD had come down at this place from a small town which had a significant impact on her language being typically accented but unimpressive.

She had black wavy hair. Her eyes were almond brown. She wore a floral white dress with lots of accessories and a black bold frame, her bright and high heels showing off her toned legs. She'd put on a couple of contrast bands and bracelets round her wrists and an axe pendant hung around her neck.

"The son of Gavalgan", said Om Shastri.

Abhilash at once started pondering over the name and spoke slowly as he did so, *"I have heard this name before"*.

"Anyways," Shahista went on.

"What other names do you have Mr. Shastri?"

"Sushen, Vishnu Gupt", Om Shastri replied as a smile crossed his face.

"What did you do as them?" Shahista emphasized.

"I taught and treated people".

"What else?"

"I worked as the chief adviser."

"Whom did you work for?"

Om Shastri was silent for a moment and then, without a warning, contrary to the perception of the team members, who thought they had ample of time to deal with him, he woke up. Shahista, sitting close to Om Shastri, got alarmed and distanced herself from him. All others stiffened in the room. Shahista's rational mind argued this to be impossible it's not even an hour, how did he get conscious! Never in her experience of over three hundred patients had a man woken up from his hypnotism so abruptly without any sign of physical disturbance.

Dr. Batra was equally stunned and disoriented. His knowledge of medicines told him that the patient could not regain consciousness before eight hours of injection, given the dose. It had not even been an hour since Om was injected. This defied all the norms ever studied and practiced by Dr. Batra. LSD was horrified too, and was poor in hiding it. None of them had any clue, what was going on!!

Om Shastri was looking at all of them without trying to get free of the shackles that constrained him.

When he spoke his tone was calm and peaceful.

"Why am I brought here? What do you people want?"

He seemed disappointed.

Dr. Shahista didn't respond to Om Shastri's inquiry. She looked over to Dr. Srinivasan across the room. Om turned towards him too.

"You are here because there are some answers we need. What do we want? Nothing but the information you possess." Dr. Srinivasan said in his bossy tone.

"How much do you know about me?" Om continued.

"Well, Mr. Shastri, not much for now. Just that Om Shastri's not the real you, that you know someone called Banda Bahadur and Sanjay, and that you were the chief adviser as Vishnu Gupt, yet another fake name you used."

Om Shastri shut his eyes tightly and a wave of pain and sorrow crossed his face.

Dr. Batra moved close to Om to inject him again.

Om tried resisting initially and let out a scream and then said, "I am immune to midazolam, flunitrazepam, barbiturates and amobarbital. This won't help you." Om's scream called in two guards to hold him in place.

Dr. Batra concealed his astonishment hearing the names of the drugs that constituted a narcotic test from Om Shastri, and infused him the same. Om started feeling sleepy and said in a hushed voice, "I am no terrorist."

3 - DISCONNECTED DISCLOSURE

Dr. Shahista started in the direction of Om Shastri to go on with hypnotizing him. She sat comfortably in front of him and stared him in the eye. Shahista's beautiful brown eyes had the magic and the power to hypnotize a person. She didn't blink at all and spoke in a soothing voice. When she touched Om Shastri on the shoulder, he fell limp and heavy. He had almost been mesmerized when Dr. Srinivasan confronted him and said, *"I am Dr. Srinivasan Rao, a retired scientist from the National Institute of Science Communication and Information Resources. I am now leading this group."* *"I know who you are"*, were Om's last words before losing consciousness again. Dr. Srinivasan registered these odd words in his mind. *"I know who you are"* which he shouldn't have said.

"Tej, is he ready to be questioned again?" Dr. Srinivasan inquired.

Dr. Batra checked some readings in a device and said, *"Yes, sir"*.

"Dr. Shahista, find out what kind of advice did Vishnu Gupt give", commanded Dr. Srinivasan.

Om Shastri started mumbling something that everyone found hard to grab, except Abhilash and Parimal.

व्याघ्रीव तिष्ठति जरा परितर्जयन्ती
रोगाश्च शत्रव इव प्रहरन्ति देहम् ।
आयुः परिस्रवति भिन्नघटादिवाम्भः
लोकस्तथाप्यहितमाचरतीति चित्रम् ॥

"What is he babbling?" LSD snapped.

"Sanskrit", said Abhilash and Parimal in unison.

Shahista was lost in her own thoughts. Her knowledge taught her that in the state of hypnotism, the patient only replies to the voice that hypnotizes him. But Om Shastri had reacted to Dr. Srinivasan's words, violating one of the most believed principles of Hypnotism.

Parimal, 35, who hailed from a village called Wardha in Maharashtra, where his father worked as a farmer, was an introvert by nature. He did PhD in Indian history. His knowledge was immeasurable in his subject. But he lacked the guts to put it forth confidently; the reason for lack of confidence was his stammering, which has been the biggest hurdle for him to keep up with others. And so, was often ignored by people. As a consequence of his silence, his presence or absence was indistinguishable.

Parimal was two inches short of six feet, creamy skinned, and handsome. He wore a checkered brown shirt with a pair of black jeans and white sport shoes. He had coal black eyes and hair in the same hue with some oil applied to it.

Parimal was refused the importance he desired in the team, owing to the fact that his questions and suggestions were naïve.

"Sanskrit! Who understands Sanskrit in this century? Let alone speak!" LSD remarked in frustration.

"Sushen!" said Abhilash to himself slowly.

"What?" asked LSD after overhearing Abhilash.

"Nothing" said Abhilash bringing himself back.

LSD insisted. *"No. I heard you repeated the name this guy said minutes ago."*

Abhilash replied. *"Sushen"*

"Yaa, that name. What is it? Tell me."

"Sushen is a very rarely used name. As per my knowledge Sushen was the name of a medic in ramayan who saved Lakshaman, the younger brother of Lord Ram in the battle with the great king Ravana by signifying a herb called sanjivni which was seldom found in the himalayas. Lord Hanuman was ordered by Lord Ram to bring sanjivni, as advised by Sushen. Lord Hanuman after reaching the Himalayas could not make the difference between sanjivni and

other herbs and so he lifted the entire mountain and flew back to Kanyakumari with it to let Sushen himself make the choice."

"Yes! I have seen the Hindu mythological picture of Hanuman flying with the mountain. Is that what you are referring to? "Yes" said Abhilash.

"Everything is unusual about him. Not even close to anything I have witnessed before", Dr. Shahista said, still lost at sea.

She then turned to Dr. Srinivasan, breaking her reverie, and asked politely, *"Sir, we should at least clearly know what we are dealing with?"*

Everyone looked at Srinivasan, expecting a fair answer.

"This is what you are here for", retaliated their boss, *"So concentrate on your work and get more out of him to help us understand what we are dealing with"*, Dr. Srinivasan glared at Shahista.

That was rude and Shahista didn't like it, as was evident from her expression. Everyone got back to the task at hand.

Parimal walked towards Dr. Batra and asked frantically, *"Dr. Batra! A…a….are you a..a..alright?"*

Dr. Batra was clearly disturbed. He gathered himself and came up with, *"Huh? Yes? yes"*

"We a..aare not much of a…an a……cquaintance. But we a…..are to work a….as a team here. You seem a bit disoriented. Is everything a……lright?" Parimal repeated in an anxious tone.

Dr. Batra felt comfortable by this kind gesture of Parimal and whispered into his ears, *"This man woke up within an hour!"*

"So?" Parimal was confused.

"How could he? That's not possible!" Dr. Batra exclaimed with his eyes wide.

"Not possible? What do you mean? We a…all saw him wake up!" Parimal went on with his innocent queries.

"Exactly" That is what's bothering me, Parimal. A single dosage of that drug takes a man down for four to five hours at the least. You know what? He didn't lose his consciousness in a dose! Then I increased it to twice the normal measure. He went dizzy for a while but still was awake. I gave him one more round as such. A dose of such kind is more than enough to kill a man. And he managed to regain his wits within an hour!" Dr. Batra went on explaining.

"This is a question mark on my knowledge and caliber. I need to find out how the hell did that happen." said the determined Dr. Batra.

Whatever Dr. Batra said didn't register on the radar of Parimal's brain. And so, he got out of it with, *"Did you tell this to Dr. Sriniv….asan?"*

"Yes, I did. Probably Dr. Srinivasan knows things we aren't aware of. When Dr. Shrinivasan and I were bringing him here, Om Shastri called Dr. Srinivasan by his nick name, Chinna!"

"How did he know it?" Parimal was shocked.

"That's the point. How on Earth could he know it?"

"He was called 'Prof. Google' in the school he was teaching in recently. His students and colleagues said that he knew everything and that he is a genius", preceded Dr. Batra.

"Google?" Bullshit! He knows Dr. Sriniv.....asan's nick n... ame, he is 'Prof. Google', ...and claims he doesn't remember his own n......ame?"

"Are you on a mission?" Shahista was all ears again.

"Yes", Om Shastri nodded.

Everyone's face went pale.

The deep lines on Dr. Srinivasan's forehead said it all about his thoughts.

LSD grew a bit tensed, thinking about interrogating a terrorist, who was being given such an importance that people who were the best from different walks of life were brought together, here in this isolated facility. Dr. Shahista was equally frightened for once.

"I knew it already! He is a Muslim. He looks like one!", snapped proud Abhilash. He had this habit of discriminating people on the basis of castes and religions. Shahista chose to ignore him and went on.

"What is your mission?"

"Hide and be hidden"

"What?"

"My belongings"

"Where do you secure it?"

"In my memories and a locker."

"Whom do you protect it for?"

"For this mankind", Om said it with a heavenly smile on his lips.

Without being questioned further, Om breathed, *"No, I am not a terrorist!"*

Shahista had lost her patience. She turned towards everyone else and discovered they were in the same boat, equally jolted. Dr. Srinivasan was on the phone talking to someone. He saw Shahista's face and hung up the phone before snapping, *"What happened?"*

"I didn't put up a question and still he spoke! Who on Earth asked him about being a terrorist?" cried Shahista, clearly taken aback.

"Lisa Samuel Dicosta", Om replied.

"I was talking to Parimal about the possibility of him being a terrorist. But I wasn't so loud", admitted LSD.

Parimal nodded in agreement.

"How come he heard you and not me?" Shahista's face grew serious with contemplation.

LSD didn't know what to say, so she kept quiet for once.

It was noon already when Om Shastri broke the spell yet again. Veerbhadra looked at his watch and noted it was 1:45 pm. He went outside the room to inspect the guards. Meanwhile in the room Om locked his eyes with fear-stricken Dr. Shahista and spoke to her like a father to his daughter, "You don't have to do this to get your answers. I am by this time in your custody. You may tackle me as you wish. Go ahead without terror on your face. I will not harm anyone. And I never did. Trust me, I'll cooperate".

Shahista was at a loss for words.

Dr. Batra crossed the room towards Dr. Srinivasan and said, "I need your permission to diagnose him sir". He was more than agitated.

Dr. Srinivasan didn't take the pains to help Dr. Batra. He was preoccupied by his own work.

Shahista left Om and walked towards the group.

"Yes, Shahista?" inquired Dr. Srinivasan on seeing her approach towards them.

"Sir, I suggest we try interrogating him without the drugs and hypnotism for once", Shahista pleaded.

Dr. Batra seemed ridiculed by Shahista's request, but chose to remain silent.

"We may do that. Are you to take the responsibility of authenticating his words? Is it ensured that only the truth is spoken?" adamant Dr. Srinivasan concluded.

"But, this is not helping either", Dr. Shahista reasoned.

"Please, let me diagnose him once, sir. I want his blood sample", Dr. Tej appealed.

"He is not a laboratory rat that you can research on, Tej. I cannot allow you that privilege", was all Dr. Batra got from his high command.

Dr. Batra and Shahista looked at each other with an expression that said, *"We are in the same boat"*.

With a deep sigh, Shahista said, *"Okay sir. Then what do we have to do now?"*

Dr. Srinivasan's phone rang. He took it out from his pocket, saw the caller's identity, and grew a bit nervous.

"All of you take a short break and thereafter prepare for the next session", said Dr. Shriniwasan in a haste, before attending to the call, he strode past them out of the room.

With Dr. Srinivasan's departure came some relaxation in the atmosphere. LSD's face had a smile swept across it instantly.

Parimal looked in Abhilash's direction and then towards LSD. Dr. Batra was still having a hard time without his answers and that was troubling him. Likewise, Dr. Shahista had her gaze on Om Shastri, who was keenly observing the room around him, and the people inside it. When he looked at Shahista, she turned away. That instant, the security chief, Veerbhadra, entered the room with two other guards. He echoed in a heavy voice, *"Everyone! This way please"*, and showed the door with a sway of his hand. All of them engaged a couple of minutes in leaving the room. Veerbhadra and Om Shastri were to be alone in the room for an hour.

The next room was occupied by the investigators. Dr. Tej was speaking to his family in his native tongue. Parimal, LSD and Abhilash were sitting comfortably round a wooden table. Dr. Shahista chose being alone for the time being. She sat on another table, scribbling something in a diary.

Parimal was struggling with his words, LSD with her wires and Abhilash in his pride were engaged in a conversation, talking about their careers and themselves.

"Why don't you join us Dr. Shahista? Let's know each other a bit", LSD invited.

"Sure! I'll be there in 5 minutes", replied the congenial woman.

Since Shahista was senior to all of them, she knew all about them from their files. She joined the crew she would be working with but she didn't know for how long. She came and sat on the empty seat which was beside Abhilash. As Dr Shahista got seated, Abhilash stood up and went on the other side changing his seat with Parimal. Everyone noticed the discrimination and felt it straight and clear but no one said anything. Dr Shahista was embarrassed.

Dr. Batra was still all ears on his phone.

"What's that diary all about?" asked LSD outspokenly, pointing towards the diary in Shahista's hands?

"I am just keeping track of all the usual and unusual happenings of the interrogation. Proves to be beneficial in a case studying later", replied Shahista with her calm smile.

"Wh….at unusual ha….appenings?" Parimal questioned in his typical manner.

"You see, he doesn't ask the usual questions. When he wakes up, he asks worriedly about what and who are we, and so on as if he already knew in his heart that he is going to be caught someday".

"M…..aybe he had experienced this before. M…..aybe he knows wh…at we are looking for", Parimal proposed.

"Even we aren't fortunate enough to know what we are looking for from him", Shahista said in a disgusted tone.

"Wha…..t other unusual tra….aits does he ss..show?" Parimal stammered.

"He breaks the spell I cast upon him without any prior sign of breaking it. It's a swift process. As if he was normally sleeping. Snap! And he wakes up", Shahista explained with a click of her finger.

"Dr. Ba…..atra is also more than concerned a….about his aa….bility to overcome over the effect of his drugs that usua….ally lasts several hours", Parimal remarked.

"I personally dread Dr. Batra's presence. Wonder why he is always infuriated and worked up!" admitted LSD.

"Dr. Batra is a nice man. He is crawling alone through the shadows. That's all", Shahista explained.

"Ohh…You know him personally?" LSD kept on.

"Yes. We have worked together earlier."

"So? What's troubling him?"

"This is not his usual self. Actually, he is a bit down in the dumps because his wife is on the death bed. Though, he is a renowned

doctor, there is not much he can do about it, that's the reason for his disappointment", said Shahista in an empathetic voice.

LSD criticized her heart for not trying to understand a situation prior of forming an opinion. And at the same time she envied Shahista of doing the same thing so easily.

There was silence for a while as Shahista pondered over the mental agony which Dr. Batra might be suffering.

A wise man comes out of a trouble wiser than before. Dr. Batra is a wise man indeed, thought Shahista.

"Abhilash, what did Om Shastri say in Sanskrit?", Shahista reinvented the conversation.

"It was a shloka (verse) I didn't fully understand it. But I think he was talking about man's life shrinking with the smooth and speedy passage of time, and he wonders something. I couldn't take it in as he spoke it in a voice too weak to reach me. But if I get to hear it once more, I can let you know the exact translation".

"I can do that easily. I can make him repeat", informed Shahista confidently.

"We must record it all for future. Shouldn't we?" suggested LSD.

"What! A..a aren't we recording it a....already?", Parimal's surprise was evident in his eyes.

At that moment, Dr. Tej joined in the group and sat with his head in his palms.

"No", replied Shahista.

"Why?" Parimal was shocked beyond explanation.

"Because Dr. Srinivasan does not want anything to be recorded", Dr. Batra interjected.

"And we are following that?" Parimal ceased being respectful.

"Yes. Because he is the boss", LSD said (eyes rolling)

"I don't think he is", Abhilash contemplated.

"What do you mean?" LSD asked.

"What I want to say is simple and straight. I think all of us, including Dr. Srinivasan, are working for someone else", Abhilash said in a secret breaking tone.

Dr. Batra and Shahista exchanged glances and before anyone could pay heed to Abhilash's intuition, Dr. Batra interrupted with, *"LSD, could you get me some information about someone?"*

"Sir, with the equipments and devices I am provided with in here, I can practically give you any information about anyone.......their account numbers, passwords, emails, places visited, current location, phone numbers, personal details.......every piece of data since they were born", replied LSD confidently as her eyes shone.

"Ok then. Dig everything you can about this man called Om Shastri", said Dr. Batra with a hint of satisfaction.

Om and Veerbhadra had been together in the room for quite some time. Om was tied up as earlier; no change in his position, and Veerbhadra was sitting idle on one of the tables. Om Shastri finally broke the silence saying, *"Can I get a glass of water, Mr. Veerbhadra?"* his voice was husky, Veerbhadra noticed. Maybe because of the dry throat he must be having, he thought.

"Get him a glass of water", he ordered one of the guards without moving at all.

"So? Since how long have you been working here?" Om tried to start up a conversation.

"It's been a while", came a flat and rude reply from Veerbhadra.

Om inhaled deeply and started smiling.

"What do you smile at?" Veerbhadra asked, irritated.

"It's going to rain soon. And I love the smell and the sound of it", replied Om Shastri, his gaze set upon the minimal sky visible through the ventilator.

He then gulped down the water he got from the guard.

"Rain? Now? Its summers! Have you lost it?" Veerbhadra responded.

Veerbhadra heard many footsteps in the corridor. Veerbhadra left the room again when everyone else entered. And within few seconds, everyone was back to their original position in the room. LSD was chirping with enthusiasm as she finally had something to work on. Abhilash continuously stared at Om Shastri, his expression unreadable. Om Shastri stared back. Dr. Batra was prepared for another session. Suddenly, he remembered having missed something.

He went over to LSD and said in a hushed voice, *"Om had also mentioned about a locker where he kept safe his information. Do check about that too."*

"Yes, sir", said LSD

Dr. Srinivasan was back in the lab. He began by scrutinizing it for all the team members. Dr. Shahista was absent.

"Abhilash!" called out Dr. Srinivasan.

"Look for Dr. Shahista and ask her to get here."

Abhilash nodded and went straight towards the door with a disgusted feeling, thinking why me!!! He knew where he would find the lady. As expected, Dr. Shahista was in the next room, keenly studying her notes.

"You still here?" Abhilash asked bluntly & reluctantly.

"I was just going through the notes I had prepared. This might help in the next session."

"Dr. Srinivasan is expecting you."

Shahista nodded.

Dr. Shahista and Abhilash started walking together. Just before entering the lab, Shahista said in a strict yet gentle tone, *"Abhilash, I treat people like people, and not on the basis of their caste. And I prefer to be treated in the same way.*

Am I clear?" Shahista's eyes were wide and looked with a penetrating gaze through Abhilash.

Abhilash had understood her message and gave his assent in a nod.

As they entered the lab, halfway inside, Dr. Batra was talking to Dr. Srinivasan.

"Sir, what will we do if he defies the medicines again?" Dr. Batra was anxious.

"We'll see", replied Dr. Srinivasan. Dr. Batra's words fell on deaf ears.

Dr. Srinivasan took the seat facing Om's back.

"Chinna, please don't do this. I am willing to cooperate in whatever you ask me for.", Om Shastri was almost pleading, his gaze set towards the ceiling, signaling towards Dr. Srinivasan, who in turn glanced in the direction of Dr. Shahista and Dr. Batra. Their faces conveyed the same wish.

"Please start", ordered Dr. Srinivasan, with antagonism and annoyance on his face as his ears were poked with this word Chinna…

Om was sedated again and the interrogation was set in motion.

The first question was to be for Abhilash to pay attention to and translate the answer for the others.

4 - THE NAMES FROM
THE HISTORY

"So, what did you advice as Vishnu Gupt?" began Shahista with the unconscious Om. Om repeated the same verse in Sanskrit

व्याघ्रीव तिष्ठति जरा परितर्जयन्ती
रोगाश्च शत्रव इव प्रहरन्ति देहम् ।
आयुः परिस्रवति भिन्नघटादिवाम्भः
लोकस्तथाप्यहितमाचरतीति चित्रम् ॥

Dr. Shahista was looking at Abhilash, who signaled thumbs up to her.

"Whom did you advice with the name of Vishnu Gupt?"
"Chandra Gupt Maurya."
"Why did you become Om Shastri?"
"To hide my real identity"
"From?"
"This world"

"What is your true identity?" Shahista was more than capable in finding out hidden answers.

"All my identities are true"

She noted this one mentally, *"All my identities are true"*.

"What were you doing as Om Shastri in Rewari?"

"Searching"

"Searching? For?"

"Subhash Chandra Bose"

All the colleagues looked at each other in surprise. Shahista didn't know what to ask or say further. This was getting weirder, she pondered. Finally, she took a deep breath and continued.

"Subhash Chandra Bose is dead"

"No. He is not", said Om with a firm gesture. *"Why do you think that Subhash Chandra Bose is not dead and is living by some other name?"* Shahista pressed.

"I don't think so. I know so."

Shahista rolled her eyes. This was not a point to be argued, she thought.

"Why are you searching for him?"

"Because he is Ashwatthama"

"Ashwa... What?" Shahista didn't get it.

Abhilash had started listening intently at the pronunciation of Ashwatthama and thereafter started walking towards Shahista.

"Ashwatthama", Om restated.

"Ask him which Ashwatthama he is talking about", Abhilash whispered in Shahista's ear.

"Ashwatthama, the son of Dronacharya, cursed immortal by Krishna", Om replied without Shahista's intervention.

'Krishna' was all that Shahista could grasp.

Abhilash turned to Dr. Batra, *"He is not making any sense"*.

Shahista asks, *"Who else are you looking for?"*

With a broken voice he said **Parshuram.**

Considering it non sense they continued…

"This name Vishnu Gupt maybe a codename", countered Dr. Batra, deep in thought.

"Or he might be mentally disturbed, a patient of split personality, or a little demented", he added.

"This could even be a case of reincarnation", Abhilash came back with his mythological point of view.

Dr. Batra paid no heed.

"What other names have you been using lately?" Shahista continued

"Govindlal Yadav, Bhairav Singh, Suvarna Pratap Reddy, Bankim Chandra Chakraborthy, Gursheel Singh Khullar, Vidur, Om Shastri, Nurool Ahmed, Protim Das, Vishnu Gupt, Kabir, Sushen, Jai Shankar Prasad, Madhukar Rao, Adhiraiyan", Om began as if reciting a mugged-up poem. His accent, tone, pitch, pronunciation, and facial expressions changed with every name he mouthed. 'Bhairav Singh', Nurool Ahmed, 'Gursheel Singh Khullar', and 'Suvarna Pratap Reddy' were uttered in a tone that spoke of strength and bravery. 'Bankim Chandra Chakraborthy' spoke in the typical Bengali style. 'Kabir' and 'Sushen' came with a wave of

calmness and serenity. The names seemed unending and continued with his pitch and tone changing with every uttered name.

Everyone in the room was awestruck at this event.

Shahista held her head in her hands signifying strain. Dr. Srinivasan was taken aback for the first time. LSD had jotted down all the names Om mentioned. Parimal was going through Shahista's notes. Something struck the PhD-in-history guy and he at once went to Dr. Batra while Om continued taking names in semi-conscious state of mind

"S…S..Sir, when Om used the names FF…Farkhseer, Chandra Gupt, Ba…..nda Bahadur, I believe he was talking about sometime in 300 B.C. B…b..because Vishnu Gupt was the other name of Chanakya! A…..and he was the chief a…..adviser to Chandra Gupt Maurya. You a….are welcome to perceive me as a ma…d ma…n but…" Parimal said in his usual unsure tone when he was interrupted midway.

"No, Parimal. I wouldn't take you as a madman. In fact, if he is actually talking about Chanakya, I need to confirm something about Banda Bahadur as well. Give me a moment." said Dr. Batra while excusing himself a bit to make a call.

LSD came over to Parimal, seemingly excited.

"I overheard your conversation. 300 B.C! That is 2316 years back, right? L.S.D said calculating in air. Could he possibly be a time traveler?" LSD's eyes were almost out of their sockets in her enthusiastic anticipation.

This insane idea left Parimal irritated and compelled him to reply coldly, *"He is nothing but a fra…..ud. That's what he is."*

"Biji, Sat Shri Akaal!" (Regards, mother)

Dr. Batra was talking on the phone louder than his usual self as his mother at the age of 80, had trouble hearing.

Dr Batra's voice was loud enough to be heard by all. And since the lab had grown quieter, everyone was easily and intently listening to the conversation. Even LSD stopped her work which put an end to the noise of clicking of keyboard buttons.

"Jinda reh puttar" (Long live my son)

Came an old voice from the other end.

"Ik gal dasso mainu… Banda Bahadur kaun si?"

(Tell me something… Who is Banda Bahadur?)

Asked Dr.Batra in his regional Punjabi accent.

"O puttar, Banda Singh Bahadur, Shri Guru Gobind Singh ji da gernel si",

(Son, Banda Singh Bahadur is the name of a general of our Lord Guru Gobind Singh) replied the feminine voice with a lot of respect and veneration, and a not so juvenile voice, in sync.

Dr. Batra heard other voice; he turned around to see the source, and instantly knew who said that. He was shocked to see Om replying all the questions that were being asked by him to his mother in Punjabi, and Om was considering them as they were being raised to him, even being in a high drug dose and unconscious state which was abnormal.

Dr. Batra's feet were getting unsteady now as he failed to interpret any of what was happening. He was feeling sick. He had been going through a lot already. And needed to break this crypt soon enough.

" Unna da intekaal kis tarah hua si?"

(How did he die?)

Dr. Batra asked slowly asking his mother on phone but he was observing Om instead, in surprise.

"Unna nu Mughal Badshah Farkhseer ne marwaya si"

(He was killed by Mughal Emperor).Came the voice out of his phone and from Om.

Everyone was beyond shocked. Om Shastri was talking of ancient times, they could bet, and was answering the questions in the language they were asked in......... Punjabi. But why, no one knew.

Breaking the silence, Veerbhadra entered the laboratory. He was short of breath which conveyed that he had been running.

He eyed Om Shastri once and then kept walking inside taking long strides.

" Aimi Aindi?"

(What happened?)

Asked Dr. Srinivasan in his native tongue. He did not feel right to involve everyone seeing Veerbhadra's body language.

" Varsam Padtondii"

(It's raining!) replied the fretful Veerbhadra.

"Aayite?

(So what?)

Dr. Srinivasan was already troubled enough to handle Om Shastri. He didn't want a new drama altogether.

"Atan ki gantala kritam yela telsindi?"

(How come he knew it hours before?)

Asked Veerbhadra, concerned.

Om started to say something in the same dialect.

Mellaga ushnograta mundu 2 degrees ta ggindi
Tarvata inka 5 degreel varuku taggumukham pattindi.
Gaali lo tema anapinchindi
Tadi matti suvasana, vacchindi gaali
40 kms vegam tho veestondi varsham
Varsham vastundi ani anukunnanu.

("The temperature dropped by two degrees and then another five degrees later. The winds blew at about forty kms. p/h. I could feel moisture in the breeze and could smell the wet soil. So I presumed that rains would follow") replied Om Shastri with certainty.

"What are you guys talking?" Dr. Batra intervened.

Everyone else was impatiently waiting for the answer.

Shahista knew the answer. *"Nothing"*, said Dr. Srinivasan affirming Shahista's assumption.

No one reacted or opposed. Shahista was confused again as to what to ask of Om Shastri. And so she was looking in the direction of her boss for the next command. The hour was on the verge of completion and as Dr. Batra had anticipated, Om showed signs of waking up again. The session was done. It was late afternoon.

Nothing went as planned and their old questions subsisted as new ones surfaced. Answers were few. Most of them are in the grip of people, who were deliberately hiding them.

"We need to talk", Dr. Batra approached Shahista.

"All of us need to talk", said exhausted Shahista.

Om Shastri stirred and revitalized. A crestfallen expression loomed over his face, as it dawned upon him that he had let out some more of his 'secrets'.

Dr Sriniwasan left the interrogation room and announced a short intermission while going

Dr. Batra ushered Shahista near the door and mouthed, "Meet me at the end of the lobby".

"I suggest we all meet together", Shahista responded with the same apprehension.

LSD joined them instantly, *"Sir, I have found something"*.

"Not here. Come with us", Dr. Batra escorted her.

"I'll bring the rest", Shahista called out.

Everyone left the room and Veerbhadra came in to take care of Om Shastri along with his guards.

At the end of the lobby, Shahista was the first to initiate a talk, *"Who the hell is he?"*

"The question is what the hell is he?" Dr. Batra was irked. *"LSD, what did you get?"* he demanded.

"Sir, many startling facts. To start with, I have found some bank accounts of Om Shastri. They all have a decent balance inside and are all in different states"

Abhilash was curious to know if he had so much money then why he would be teaching in a school, living a mediocre life.

"Hmm...and?" Dr. Batra listened in a rapt manner.

"All his accounts have his photograph on them as an identity. I then used his photograph as a key to dig out other information of the various names he pronounced. I discovered that Protim Das has a valid all India driving license. Govindlal Yadav has a voter identity card to his name. Bankim Chandra Chakraborthy possesses a passport; Madhukar Rao owns a lot of bonds and shares of DSP dated about seventy years ago. This is the same day when DSP was incorporated and its initial public offering was issued. These shares were purchased by Madhukar Rao's father, Mr. Venkata Ramanna Rao. The accounts possessed by Mr. Venkata Ramanna Rao have the same face as identity, Om Shastri's. Om Shasri is forty years old. His father died at the age of forty as per the records. I went through the data of the fathers of all the mentioned names. Different names, same face.

Now coming to the lockers, Gursheel Singh Khullar has a locker in Punjab National Bank, in Punjab itself; and S.P Reddy owns a locker in Andhra bank in Hyderabad. All police records are clean except for Gursheel Singh's father. Have identical face. He was caught at the Indo-Pak border. He is one of the people who were ever imprisoned in Pakistan. All of these names are educated from prestigious institutes and universities. Adhiraiyan is a doctor. B.C Chakraborthy has traveled to Paris. I didn't come across anything about Vishnu Gupt, though. Neither is Chandra Gupt associated with any of the names he mentioned. Same is the case with Vidur and Sanjay", LSD was proud of her skills in her field.

"Try Mahabharata for Vidur and Sanjay." Said Abhilash.

Before L.S.D could react to it, Dr. Batra speculated "What about his mother?"

"Their mothers all died when they were very young. No photographs could be found. All of these names have been raised by single fathers", LSD informed.

Which can't be a coincidence said Dr. Shahista.

"He had said that all his identities were real", Shahista contemplated.

"Did you possibly spot any connection between all these people and Subhash Chandra Bose?" asked Dr. Batra facing LSD.

"Sort off... as I ran into some really astonishing facts claimed by people who allege to possess information regarding Subhash Chandra Bose", LSD revealed.

"That he didn't die in a plane crash? Everyone knows that", Parimal questioned in a stammering tone. (His eyes were filled with anxiety).

"Yes. But apart from that, I unearthed something very weird. Subhash Chandra Bose died five times, with five different names, *in five different cities in India"*, LSD spoke as if revealing a skeleton in the cupboard.

"What?" everyone screamed all together.

"Huh, that was imminent. This man inside attracts everything unworldly to himself", Dr. Batra denigrated.

LSD smiled at the joke.

Subhas Chandra Bose was born on 23 January 1897, was an Indian nationalist whose disobedient patriotism made him a hero in India, but whose attempt during World War II to liberate India of British rule with the help of Nazi Germany and Imperial Japan left a troubled inheritance. The honorific Netaji, (Hindustani: "Respected Leader") was earlier

a leader of the younger, fundamental, wing of the Indian National Congress in the late 1920s and 1930s, rising to become Congress President in 1938 and 1939. However, he was expelled from Congress leadership positions in 1939 following differences with Mahatma Gandhi and the Congress high command. He was subsequently placed under house arrest by the British before escaping from India in 1940.

"Subhash Chandra Bose was believed to be dead in August 1945 at Tayhiko Pharmosa (now Taiwan) in a plane crash. In the unanimity of intellectual opinion, Subhas Chandra Bose's death occurred from third-degree burns. However, many among his supporters, especially in Bengal, refused at the time, and have refused since, to believe either the fact or the circumstances of his death. Conspiracy theories appeared within hours of his death and have thereafter had a long shelf life,

keeping alive various fierce myths about Bose. These myths of Bose being yet alive got strength soon after, when in 1945 itself, he was seen in Delhi and believed to be murdered at Red Fort. But, 15 years later in 1960 he was sighted in a photograph that was captured in Paris.

Bankim Chandra Chakraborthy happened to be in Paris in 1964 in search of Subhash Chandra Bose. On 27th May 1964, Subhash Chandra Bose was seen at the funeral of Jawahar Lal Nehru. He was again claimed to be dead as a saint in 1977 by someone. People said he lived in Shivpuklam in Madhya Pradesh and was reduced to ashes at the same place. After all this humbug and mystification, surfaced a theory of Gumnami Baba. (A saint who is anonymous.) He addressed his people from behind the curtains. In Faizabad, Uttar Pradesh, Gumnami baba's confidants somehow revealed about his having traveled to Germany in 1944; the same time when Subhash Chandra Bose is said to have met Adolf Hitler in Germany.

His confidants let out that he praised the beauty of Paris every now and then. There exists no record confirming Gumnami baba's visit to Paris. But Subhash Chandra Bose had definitely put his foot there. Gumnami baba's close friends say that whenever aspersions were heard about him being Subhash Chandra Bose, he used to change his residence.

He is believed to have left his body on 16th September 1985. Though, another point of interest lies not in this date but in his date of birth, which coincidentally happens to be 23rd January 1897, the same day that Subhash Chandra Bose was born. Needless to say, our subject is of the opinion that Subhash Chandra Bose is still alive and furthermore, he is searching for him", LSD laid out all the facts and information she had laid her hands on.

Everyone was quiet for a moment, comprehending, putting together all the pieces, decoding again. But nothing made sense. After a while, Dr. Batra spoke up, *"Abhilash, what did that shloka (verse) mean?"*

> *"Old age frightens man like a tiger;*
> *Diseases strike the body like enemies*
> *Life drips down as water from a broken pot;*
> *Yet people think of harming others;*
> *They do not realize that they are transitory;*
> *This is indeed a matter of wonder."*

Abhilash answered in the typical tone of a priest reciting a verse.

"That is the exact meaning of the verse", he continued with egotism.

"None of us are aware of the direction we are heading in through this interrogation. But there is a person who has all our answers and it's about time we should know the purpose we all are serving here. I am going to Dr. Srinivasan. I'll come back with the answers, or I'll leave from here right now. Is anyone joining me?" asked Dr. Batra, resolute in his decision.

5 - OPEN ENDS

In the lab, Veerbhadra and Om Shastri were forced into each other's company yet again. Veerbhadra had questions that clouded him, but he couldn't talk to Om. A tiny mistake could put him on the verge of dismissal, he thought. And so he deliberately kept alive the state of uneasiness he was in.

Om had been observing Veerbhadra since he had entered.

"You alright?" Om asked, concerned.

"Yes! Why?" Veerbhadra replied, shattering his daydream.

"You look stressed", Om said.

Veerbhadra was in dilemma whether to put forward or dodge the thing that was bothering him. He remained silent for a few seconds, contemplating. But the urge to know was far more intense than everything else.

And so he asked, *"You are seated in a chamber. How could you possibly know that it will rain and that too hours before the weather built up? Moreover, you calculated the wind speed, smelt the wet soil, felt the altering temperature. There was no wind in the room.*

How can your senses be that strong! How did you do that?"

Veerbhadra was moving his head sideways, in disbelief.

Om Shastri smiled a bit.

"As a matter of fact, I am also aware that I am sitting in an island on the Southern coast of India. And I just make it out with the help of my senses." Om said as if skills like these were an insignificant part of him.

Veerbhadra was shocked beyond his senses.

"You can't know that! You were unconscious, and blindfolded in the container when you were brought here!"

"Well, but I do know all of it. It just needs experience and practice. Even you can do that. Anyone can. ", Om shrugged in a matter of fact way.

"How?" Veerbhadra was unable to take in any of this.

"As you can easily differentiate between numerous colors with your eyes, just focus, smell in layers. Likewise you can see an airplane vanishing in the sky after it takes off, and an eagle transforms into a dot while it moves higher. The same way you can smell things coming close, and going further." Om explained, betraying all logics and reasoning Veerbhadra had ever learnt.

Veerbhadra had much to resolve, and so, not waiting for his brain to comprehend what had just been told, he put up another question saying, *"You are not a South Indian. How do you speak such fluent and flawless Telugu?"*

"When did I speak in Telugu?" Om was mystified.

Both of them now stared at each other, perplexed. And before anyone could reply, Dr. Srinivasan entered the room. Coincidentally, Dr. Batra also followed in. Veerbhadra first looked at Dr. Srinivasan and then towards Dr. Batra.

Dr. Batra arrogantly stared in the direction of Om Shastri, and then murmured to Dr. Srinivasan, *"Sir, we want to talk to you."*

"We?" Asked Dr Sriniwasan

"All of us, sir."

"Not now. We'll talk after this session, at the lunch break."

"We will not begin another session before talking to you, sir." Dr. Tej emphasized.

"Where is the rest of the team?" Dr. Srinivasan snapped hysterically.

"In your office, waiting for both of us", Dr. Batra told.

Om and Veerbhadra were looking at both of them and listening to their conversation. Dr. Srinivasan banged a file on the table, exasperated, and proceeded towards Dr. Batra. Dr. Batra turned the other way and left the room. Dr. Srinivasan turned around on his way and signaled Veerbhadra to follow him. Veerbhadra followed unwillingly. The guards were left behind to keep an eye on Om Shastri.

"The temperature of the oil is rising! The chopped onions will burn even with a slight delay." Om called out from behind Veerbhadra, a smile stretched across his face.

Veerbhadra left the room behind Dr. Srinivasan, on his way Inspite of entering Dr Sriniwasan's cabin; he reached out to peep inside the kitchen, just to make sure. He was astonished to see the flame burning with a bulk fryer over it and the chef out of sight. Chopped onions were kept beside the stove for frying in the bulk fry. The oil had reached the appropriate temperature. Veerbhadra reached out and overturned the vessel of onions in the pan. The chef suddenly appeared and was stunned to see Veerbhadra there. Veerbhadra, on the other hand, left the kitchen in a haste to follow up Dr. Srinivasan.

Dr. Srinivasan entered his office and found everyone standing there. He took his chair behind the table, and sat down in a habitual fashion, with an attitude of superiority. He kept his gaze on Dr. Batra. The tension in the room was tangible which heated up the environment.

"Who is he?" Dr. Batra began with the obvious question.

"Tej, you are here to do what you have been called for. You haven't been called to question me."

"I have the right to know. Who is the man we are dealing with?" Dr. Batra pushed his limits further as he was power backed by the team.

Dr. Srinivasan was offended and stood up immediately, saying, *"No! You do not have any rights here. All your rights are reserved with me."*

"Please calm down, sir", Shahista interjected at Dr. Srinivasan's burst, and continued. *"There are some strange*

conclusions we are being compelled to draw on the basis of our incomplete knowledge of him. And we all are alarmed and confused."

Shahista's words calmed Dr. Srinivasan to an extent, and he replied, "None of you need to be afraid. You are all safe here."

Veerbhadra, who was standing right behind Dr. Srinivasan, nodded in agreement.

"We may be safe here. But our families might not be, if he is a terrorist." Dr. Batra showed his concern.

"He is not a terrorist damn it!" Dr. Srinivasan got worked up yet again, and thundered in his throaty voice. His verdict seemed to be echoing in the distance.

"How can you be so sure?" Dr. Batra wasn't giving in to someone's whims and tantrums. Not this time.

"I know that", Dr. Srinivasan was clearly controlling himself, folding his hands on his chest.

"What more do you know?" Dr. Batra demanded, doing the same thing in return.

Dr. Srinivasan remained tight lipped. Shahista came close to Dr. Srinivasan, consoled him by patting on his shoulder and made him sit down. She offered him a glass of water that was kept on the table. He took it.

Shahista allowed the man to relax before saying very calmly, "Sir, we have come across some facts which is bothering us leading to such open-ended conclusions. LSD, please brief sir about it."

LSD iterated the gist of her knowledge about Om Shastri by saying, *"Sir, this man we recognize as Om Shastri has many identities in various parts of the country. Somewhere he is mentioned as his own father, and somewhere as his own son, carrying the same face but different names. I came across two active lockers in the names of his other identities and numerous bank accounts with huge sums residing in them. Nearly, he came out as a clean person in terms of legality. He seems a highly organized person and might be working for some underground terrorist organization. He is into a highly confidential mission, which we have not discovered yet. Other fact we caught hold on is that he is searching for Subhash Chandra Bose, which may be of utmost concern to the government authorities and to the nation at large."*

Dr. Srinivasan intently listened as LSD presented the facts, with attention.

Dr. Shahista taking it from there said, *"While in the state of hypnotism, he talked of people who walked the Earth in the past millenniums. Some of us suppose that he remembers all his reincarnations. Some think he might be a patient of split personality disorder. He could even be a member of some ancient secret group working generation after generation, on some hidden purpose. But none of his identities stands in coherence with any of these possibilities."*

As Dr. Shahista finished, a silence swept the workplace. Shahista went on…

"Sir, help us with what you know if you want us to help you".

"What is this facility behind the scenes? Why did we get this man? What are we struggling to bring out of him? Tell us all you

know, please Sir", Dr. Batra sounded more helpless than enraged this time.

Dr. Srinivasan didn't let any expression crowd his face, as usual. He took in a deep breath and stared at his feet, as if calculating something in his head.

After a while, he spoke.

"Okay. I'll tell you all whatever I know. But before I do that, I want you to fetch me with the details of the lockers Om mentioned".

LSD says, *"already done sir, here it is".*

LSD willingly handed over the page to Dr. Shrinivasan, who passed it on to Veerbhadra.

Veerbhadra left the room with the paper, instantly. He knew what to with it.

Dr. Srinivasan carefully unlocked a vault in his desk, and took out a few photographs and some documents. He handed all of it to Dr. Shahista, who in turn circulated parts of it to the others, after having a look at them one by one. All photographs captured Om Shastri in contrasting appearances and outfits. Each snapshot contained the year and the place where it was taken. Shahista read them one by one-1874 in Banaras, 1882 in Haryana, 1888 in Madras, 1895 in Maharashtra, 1902 in Kerala, 1916 in Lucknow, 1930 at the salt *satyagraha*(a request for truth-the movement lead by Mahatma Gandhi for complete independence), 1944 in the forward block of Subhash Chandra Bose's army. 1947 in the crowd at the flag hoisting, 1964 at Jawaharlal Nehru's funeral, 1984 at Smt.

Indira Gandhi's funeral, 1991 at Rajiv Gandhi's funeral, 1998/2001/2005/2010/2011/2012/2013/2014/2015…

Dr. Srinivasan carefully studied their faces and said, *"These are the death certificates and other governmental records proving the deaths of all those names carried by Om. But, once he is dead somewhere, he gets alive somewhere else. Remarkably, he has donned the same age in each photograph, neither younger nor older. Approximately forty years."* Dr. Srinivasan paused for the information to be grasped by all of them, and when he spoke again, his voice was intense.

"That is why all of you are here. And you aren't called here to question me as to who the man is, rather I am here to get answers from you about this man. You all are a part of this secret mission to get answers and relevant information from this mysterious man. Remember, SECRET MISSION!.

Dr. Batra had his mind flooded with a lot of doubts, and he didn't cease to put them forward.

"Who owns this organization?" he asked bluntly.

"Enough questions, Tej!. This is all you needed to know. Now you are left with only two choices. Get back to work or pack your belongings and I shall make arrangements for your return." Dr. Srinivasan warned, unable to hide the scorn in his voice.

Dr. Tej was still, and about to turn on his heels to get back to the laboratory, when Shahista spoke up.

"Sir, it will take weeks together to gather all the information from Om Shastri as he regains his wits every other hour of hypnotizing."

"Can you suggest some other way, doctor?" Dr. Srinivasan asked as if he knew the answer.

"Yes sir. I suggest we should try talking to him directly without any use of sedatives or hypnotism", Shahista proposed.

"I'm afraid he won't speak anything that way", Dr. Srinivasan showed some concern.

"He will, sir. He has no idea as to how much he has already disclosed. We can make him believe that we know everything, and then he would answer everything consciously."

"This could prove to be a risky procedure for all of you", Dr. Srinivasan warned.

Dr. Shahista had begun to learn convincing and handling Dr. Srinivasan. Her understanding approach had the strength to win over his dominant personality. So, she said, *"Sir, I have interrogated numerous criminals. And my experience can very well assure you that he is not to be feared."*

"I don't think we should trust him without the drugs and hypnotism. There would always be a possibility of the truth being doctored with while it travels through his nerves to his mouth", Dr. Srinivasan maintained his stand on the issue.

"We could make use of a lie detector and LSD here would help us in visualizing everything that he thinks while he speaks", Dr. Batra spoke as if letting out some million dollar plan.

"Sir, a few wires would run from his head to the monitor, and we would be able to receive the wavelength of his thoughts and convert them to the visuals on the screen, thereby seeing the exact replica of what he imagined, along with the minutest details like the era and the time. Am I right, LSD?" Shahista said.

"That will be great fun!" LSD chimed in excitement. Her words came out a bit fumbled as she had her mouth occupied by a chewing gum, which she wasn't embarrassed of. But right after she said that, everyone else threw a glance at her that said *"What's wrong with you?"* In a response to this gesture, she stopped chewing her gum, and started working silently.

"Sir, words may lie, but thoughts can't be voluntarily controlled. If we set the visuals of his thoughts, there's no way he can fool us around", Shahista said.

Dr. Srinivasan went back and forth in his mind, weighing everything against the possible consequences while everyone else waited for an indication.

Shahista pleaded, *"Sir, it's your chance to believe in us, and in your own selection of the best experts"*.

Dr. Srinivasan was forced to agree to it. But before he did that, he asked, *"What if this doesn't work?"*

"Then we will carry on the same way we have been doing until now", Dr. Batra assured.

"Sir, it has been very difficult until now. Every sentence he spoke stimulated numerous questions. I am now clueless about what to ask him", Shahista said.

"Okay, go ahead with whatever you feel like. But be cautious, Shahista. You must maintain the necessary distance. No recordings. We'll start after the lunch." Dr. Srinivasan was concerned.

Everyone proceeded towards the dining for lunch. But Dr. Shahista headed towards the laboratory.

She walked towards Om, and stood in front of him. She brought back the jovial smile on her lips, and said, *"Hello. I am Shahista. I didn't get a chance to introduce myself properly before.*

Om, please have your lunch meanwhile I'll join others. If you need anything do let me know." Shahista tried to befriend Om, as her job after lunch was to talk to him in his consciousness. Psychology says that once you gain the trust of a person you get his secrets too.

I requested them to untie me, *I wanted to use the restroom,* said Om humbly. *"Ohh.sure Om. Actually, they aren't authorized to talk to you or make any decision on their own. Please pardon the inconvenience."* Shahista said with hospitality on her face.

She then ordered one of the guards to escort Om Shastri to the restroom.

Shahista was now confident for the next session as Om wasn't defensive or rude to her.

As the guard did the needful, Om turned and said *"One more thing, I'm a vegetarian and I don't like Cabbage either, Potatoes and pulses would work. Green chilli and salt separately, please"*, Om laid out his eating style.

Shahista didn't understand him but nodded. She then left the laboratory and as she reached the dining room and saw the menu, she was freaked out. She saw non-vegetarian food being served, and two vegetables-potato, and cabbage. She got hold of herself and said, *"Do not send non-vegetarian for Om, neither cabbage. He doesn't eat that."*

"How do you know?" LSD was baffled.

"He told me himself", Shahista replied.

"What?" LSD enquired.

"That he is a vegetarian and he dislikes cabbage. And that he wants green chillies and salt separately."

Everyone looked at each other in shock while Shahista started having her food.

LSD started racking her brain, and spoke slowly, *"How could he make it out that potatoes and cabbage are in the menu for the lunch. Moreover, if he stated that he is a vegetarian, how did he know that even non-vegetarian food has been cooked?"*

Shahista stopped midway listening to that, and got lost in deep thoughts.

Everyone else present was silent with no theories to support the far-fetched act.

6 - DIVINE YUGAS

There was a momentary silence after which Parimal spoke, *"Looking at all the photogra.....phs, the theories of his split persona....lity or reincarna...tion are disca..rded. What's the new expla..nation?"*

Another few moments passed in silence, which was shattered by LSD, saying, *"Time travelling!"*

She was into her laptop when she said that, concentrating in her gadgets.

"Bah! Humbug! Time travelling is a myth. Time is not stagnant so that you can travel back and forth over it. The past is past and the future hasn't materialized yet." Abhilash criticized the theory of LSD.

LSD chose to ignore his words Dr. Batra then orated to everyone, *"Parimal says that Vishnu Gupt, which Om claims he himself is, was the other name of Chanakya. And also that Chandra Gupt is probably Chandra Gupt Maurya of the Maurya Dynasty.*

I am compelled to trust him because the Banda Singh Bahadur and Farqseer he mentioned are names from the Sikh mythology. You all might have overheard my conversation on the phone few minutes ago. Now I want to know your views about all this".

"Dr. Tej, you are a doctor. How could you believe all this? This is downright illogical", Shahista was in a fury.

"Okay, Dr. Shahista. Then please proceed and logically justify all these people and their fathers carrying the same face in the documents LSD discovered", Dr. Batra retorted.

Dr. Shahista was speechless and remained so.

"Sir, the recitation by Om Shastri is an original by Chanakya", LSD was still on her mission.

Who is Banda Bahadur? And whats the past of Chanakya? Abhilash questioned.

"Chanakya's birth is believed to be in 350 BCE but is a matter of controversy, and there are multiple theories about his origin. According to the Buddhist text, his birthplace was Takshashila. The Jain scriptures, mention him as a Dramila, implying that he was a

native of South India.According to another Jain belif Chanakya was born in the Chanaka village of the Golla region, to a Brahmin named Chanin and his wife Chaneshvari.Other sources mention his father's name as Chanak and state that Chanakya's name is derived from his father's name. According to some sources, Chanakya was a Brahmin from North India, scholar in Vedas and a devotee of Vishnu. According to Jain accounts he became a Jain in his old age like Chandragupta Maurya." Described Parimal

"Chanakya was an Indian teacher, philosopher, economist, jurist and royal advisor. He is traditionally identified as Kauṭilya or Vishnu Gupta, who authored the ancient Indian political treatise, the Arthashastra. As such, he is considered the pioneer of the field of political science and economics in India, and his work is thought of as an important precursor to classical economics. His works were lost near the end of the Gupta Empire and not rediscovered until 1915." Everyone gave full attention to Parimal's narration about Chanakya.

L.S.D took over from there with her laptop reading about more information on him.

"Originally a teacher at the ancient university of Takshashila, Chanakya assisted the first Mauryan emperor Chandragupta in his rise to power. He is widely credited for having played an important role in the establishment of the Maurya Empire. Chanakya served as the chief advisor to both Emperors Chandragupta and his son Bindusara."

"According to one legend, Chanakya discharged to the jungle and starved himself to death. According to another legend mentioned

by the Hemachandra, Chanakya died as a result of a conspiracy by Subandhu, one of Bindusara's ministers. Subandhu, who did not like Chanakya, told Bindusara that Chanakya was responsible for the murder of his mother. Bindusara asked the nurses, who confirmed the story of his birth. Bindusara was horrified and enraged. When Chanakya, learned that the King was angry with him, he decided to end his life. In accordance with the Jain tradition, he decided to starve himself to death. By this time, the king had found out the full story which was that Chanakya was not responsible for his mother's death, which was an accident. He asked Subandhu to convince Chanakya to give up his plan to kill himself. However, Subandhu instead conducted a ceremony for Chanakya only to burn him alive. There are no definite mentions of Chanakya's death".......
Abhilash spoke in between saying *"which means Chanakya's death is still incomplete"*

"Chanakya is regarded as a great scholar and envoi in India. Many Indian nationalists regard him as one of the earliest people who imagined the united India spanning the entire subcontinent. India's former National Security Advisor Shiv Shankar Menon praised Chanakya's Arthashastra for its clear and precise rules which apply even today." L.S.D continued again.

Banda Bahadur?? questioned Abhilash again.

Everyone looked at Dr Batra's face for some light on this Sikh name. Dr Batra stated,

Banda Singh Bahadur was born in 1970 with the name of Lachman Das and later became a Sikh military commander.

At age 15 he left home to become a severe and was given the name "Madho Das". He established a monastery at Nanded, on the bank of the river Godavarī, where in 1708 he was visited by, and became a disciple of, Guru Gobind Singh, who gave him the new name of Banda Singh Bahadur. Equipped with the blessing and authority of Guru Gobind Singh, he assembled a fighting force and led the struggle against the Mughal Emperor. After establishing his authority in Punjab, Banda Singh Bahadur abolished the zamindari system, and granted property rights to the tillers of the land. In 1715 Banda Singh Bahadur was captured from the Gurdas Nangal fort and put in an iron cage. The remaining Sikhs were captured and chained. The Sikhs were brought to Delhi in a procession with the 780 Sikh prisoners, 2,000 Sikh heads hung on spears, and 700 cartloads of heads of slaughtered Sikhs used to terrorize the population. They were put in the Delhi fort and pressurized to give up their faith and become Muslims. On their firm refusal all of them were ordered to be executed. Every day, 100 Sikhs were brought out of the fort and murdered in public, which went on for around seven days. The Mughals could hardly contain themselves of joy while the Sikhs showed no sign of dejection or humiliation, instead they sang their sacred hymns; none feared death or gave up their faith. After 3 months of confinement, in June 1716 Banda Singh's eyes were gouged, his limbs were severed, his skin removed, and later killed.

LSD had her head ducked into her laptop again and was clicking and scrolling continuously.

"Sir, there is huge time gap between the lifetimes of Chanakya and Banda Bahadur. Chanakya belonged to the era of 350 B.C,

whereas *Banda Singh Bahadur belonged to a more recent period of history that is 1675"*, LSD spoke, her eyes affixed on her screen.

"But Om Shastri said he worked as an advisor to both. Maintained a difference of 2000 years almost! What rubbish!" Shahista flayed.

"He i….s not referring to divergent centuries. He is ta….lking of way different millenniums. How is that pos….sible?" Parimal put forth.

"I would say he is talking about the various Yugas. He somewhere indicated the name Sanjay, the son of Gavalgan. LSD, would you please search this through the Hindu mythology, especially the period around Mahabharat?" Abhilash joined in carrying his usual proud self.

"Yugas? Abhilash, explain", LSD countered sarcastically.

"My dear, that is impossible for you to grasp", Abhilash snapped back with an even more sarcastic smile.

"Still you ought to explain to us", Dr. Shahista interjected.

Dr. Shahista and LSD waited for Abhilash to begin and had their gaze on him."

"The Hindu mythology bifurcates time into four Yugas. These are Satya Yuga, Treta Yuga, Dwapara Yuga, and Kali Yuga."

Shahista nodded, slowly comprehending.

"If at all there is a theory, how many years roughly does each of these Yugas consist of?"

Divine Yugas

Abhilash picks up a pen and paper and starts writing while answering Shahista's question.

"According to Srimad Bhagavatam, one of the earliest known texts describing the yugas, The duration of the Satya yuga equals 4,800 years of the demigods; Treta yuga equals 3600 years, Dvapara yuga equals 2,400 years; and that of the Kali yuga is 1,200 years of the demigods. One year of the demigods is equal to 360 years of the human beings. These 4 yugas follow a timeline ratio of (4:3:2:1). The duration of the yugas is therefore:

4,000 + 400 + 400 = 4,800 divine years (= 1,728,000 human years) = 1 Satya Yuga

3,000 + 300 + 300 = 3,600 divine years (= 1,296,000 human years) = 1 Tretā Yuga

2,000 + 200 + 200 = 2,400 divine years (= 864,000 human years) = 1 Dvāpara Yuga

1,000 + 100 + 100 = 1,200 divine years (= 432,000 human years) = 1 Kali Yuga.

The value of 24,000 years fits relatively close with the modern astronomical calculation of one full precession of the equinox, which takes 25,772 years. According to the beliefs, in the Satya Yuga, the process of self-realization was meditation of Vishnu. During this Yuga, majority of the population were epitomes of goodness. In the Treta Yuga, man extended his knowledge and power over the attributes of Universal Magnetism, the source of positive, negative, and neutralizing electricity, and the two poles of creative attraction

66

and repulsion. People in this age remained righteous and adhered to moral ways of life, though the Godly qualities decreased by one fourth in comparison to the Satya Yuga. Lord Rama, of the fable of Ramayana, lived in this age. In the Dwapara Yuga, the process of self-realization was the worship of deities in the temples. Godly qualities reduced to fifty percent by this age. We live in the Kali Yuga, a world infested with impurities and vices. People possessing genial virtues are diminishing day by day. Floods and famine, war and crime, deceit and duplicity characterize this age. But, say the scriptures, final emancipation can be acquired in this age only. It is predicted that at the end of Kali Yuga, Lord Shiva shall destroy the universe and all the physical bodies would undergo a great transformation. After such a dissolution, Lord Brahma would recreate the world and mankind would become the 'Beings of Truth' once again", Abhilash explained.

"How can you sum up the difference between these ages in a few words?" Shahista asked.

"The four yugas widely accepted in Hinduism are- Satya yug (The first yuga), Treta yug (Ramayana), Dwapara yug (Mahabharata), Kal yug (Present).

In Satya Yuga, the fight was between two worlds- Deva loka (pertaining to the world of Gods) and Asura loka (pertaining to the world of demons.) Asura loka, being the evil, was a different world.

In Treta Yuga, the fight was between Rama and Ravana. Both rulers from two different 'countries', evil and good in the same world.

In Dwapara Yuga, the fight was between Pandavas and Kauravas.

Both good and evil in the same 'family'. Kindly note how the evil is getting closer. For example, from a 'different world' to a 'different country' to the 'same family'.

Now, know where is the evil in Kalyug??? It is inside us. Both good and evil live within us. The battle is within us. What will emerge victorious? What will dominate the other, our inner goodness or the evil within??"

Shahista looked at him, staggered.

Before Abhilash finished, LSD had started on her new task.

"Why did you specify Mahabharat?" Shahista was quizzical.

"Because Om mentioned Vidur as one of his names, and LSD didn't find anything concerning this name", Abhilash said in a manner of letting out a secret to a kid.

"Will somebody tell me what the hell is going on here and what exactly are we dealing with?" Dr. Shahista thundered.

An eerie silence engulfed the room at Shahista's outburst and remained so until Dr. Batra spoke up.

"Abhilash, and Parimal, tell us in detail your views and thoughts".

"Has anyone here heard of Ashwatthama and Parshuram?" Abhilash was the one to reply.

"Yes", replied the innocent Parimal.

"Only heard of them, yes", Dr. Batra informed.

"Never heard of them!" Shahista muttered.

"Googled them now. Got an idea", the tech-savvy LSD replied.

"Okay. The word 'Parshu' in this name signifies an axe. Parshuram literally translates to Rama with an axe. He was the sixth avatar of Lord Vishnu, the fifth son of Renuka and the sage-Jamadagni. He is one of the seven Chiranjivis (a person who lives forever- an immortal) in Hinduism. Parshuram is mostly known for ridding the world of kshatriyas (the clan of kings and warriors) twenty-one times, after the mighty king Kartavirya killed his father. The birthplace of Bhargav Parshuram is contested, although the history of his lineage is considered to be emerging in the Haihaya kingdom located in the modern day Maheshwar, near the city of Indore in Madhya Pradesh.

He received an axe after undertaking terrible penance to please Lord Shiva, who in turn taught him martial arts. Pleased with his extreme devotion, intense desire and perpetual meditation, Lord Shiva rewarded Shri Bhargav Rama-his original name- divine weapons, which included the unconquerable and indestructible axe, Parshu, and so he was named, Parshuram. Lord Shiva had then ordered Parshuram to liberate the Earth from felons, demons and those blind with pride. Parshuram lived long enough to see the subsequent incarnations of Vishnu as Rama and Krishna. Parshuram possessed a bow of Lord Shiva given by the King of Deities, Lord Indra, who had with him the bow, called Vijaya Dhanush. In the Ramayana, Parshuram had given the bow to the father of princess Sita, King Janak, for her Swayamwar (a process of selecting the right mate and an eligible match for a princess). As a test of strength, suitors were asked to lift and string the mystic weapon. None of them was successful, except Lord Rama. But, as Lord Rama struggled to string the bow, it broke in two halves and produced tremendous sound that reached Parshuram's ears whilst he meditated atop the Mahendra mountains. Infuriated, Parshuram came to confront King Ram, who, he realized, was the incarnation of Lord Vishnu.

Parshuram has played crucial roles in the Ramayana and the Mahabharat as the mentor of Bhishma, Karna, and Drona. Drona is mostly referred to as Dronacharya. 'Acharya', meaning teacher, he was the mentor of the Kauravas- who were hundred brothers in number, and the Pandavas- who were five." Abhilash was adept at explaining concepts and facts pertaining to Hinduism.

"Now, why are we going astray? Abhilash, what is the point you are driving at?" Shahista was in no mood of listening lengthy lectures on Hinduism.

"The gist of the story is that Parshuram has appeared in every yuga and is an immmortal."

Dr. Srinivasan sat in his office, with his phone on. He addressed the person he was conversing with as "Sir". It seemed as if some orders were being passed on through the phone to Dr. Srinivasan. He assured 'Sir' the safety of the laboratory and all other members. He then explained as to why it was important to pay heed to the suggestions of the other team members.

At last he said, *"Thank you, sir"*, and hung up.

The next session begins.

7 - EXISTENCE EXHIBITED

Everyone assembled in the same room and took their respective seats. Shahista sat on the seat next to Om. She stretched her neck to make sure the guards were in the vicinity this time, for the sake of the safety of everyone. This time everybody could sense the sensitivity of the situation; they could feel something and were apprehensive.

Dr. Srinivasan came close to Om, bent down in front of him and said, *"What should we call you? Om? Or Bankim? Madhukar maybe? Gursheel is good? Or you'd prefer Vidur? Surprised right? You have spilled out a lot of things that were hidden. Now, either we bring out all of it just the same way, or you might choose to reveal willingly. By force or by choice? Either way, we will acquire whatever we desire. What do you say?"* Dr. Srinivasan had a sardonic smile.

Om didn't speak and his face told that he had already given in. He appeared to be very disturbed like someone who just told a thief where his million-dollar treasure could be found.

Dr. Srinivasan straightened up, moved farther and instructed Dr. Shahista to explain Om about the new process.

Shahista complied.

"Om, we are going to hook you up to a lie detector and also we are going to project your thoughts as visuals on the screen by matching their wavelength and converting them." Shahista spoke as humbly as she could like a mother explaining her child who's about to be vaccinated.

"Which means that..." Om said steadily and was interjected by Dr. Batra.

"Which means you can't lie, because your thoughts will be displayed as clearly as you have lived them."

"I am sure you don't have any objection. Do you?" Dr. Srinivasan spoke arrogantly.

"Do I have a choice?" Om said

"None! Dr. Batra, set up" Dr. Srinivasan geared things up.

"Yes sir." Dr. Batra replied.

Om glanced towards Shahista who was already looking at him sympathetically.

Dr. Srinivasan left the laboratory for his office and dialled up Veerbhadra's contact on his way.

"Veerbhadra, report!", he commanded.

At the other end, Veerbhadra said, *"Sir, our people have those lockers secured. They will reach here in sometime."*

Shrinivasan asks whatever is in that locker to be brought to him as soon as they arrive.

Veerbhadra responds, consider it retained sir, going through the location and address of the locker.

Shrinivasan questions how much time you need?

Veerbhadra takes a moment to calculate the travel time and informs Dr.Shrinivasan that he will have it on his desk by early morning.

Veerbhadra leaves. Shrinivasan continues talking to Dr. Batra and rest of the team members.

Outside Dr. Shrinivasan's office Veerbhadra makes some calls and arrangements in order to complete his task in the given time.

Veerbhadra (on phone) *"how long will it take to reach me?"* After hearing it from the other side, Veerbhadra says, *"Do not leave any traces behind."* My men will give you a sealed envelope. After securing it, deliver it to the address in the envelope to the person who gives you this code. 5MW580YLF written as a serial number on a 100 rupees note.

Veerbhadra disconnects the call and dials another number.

Veerbhadra (on phone) *"you will get the parcel tonight at the same address. Secure it. Your code is 5MW580YLF get the package delivered safely to the chopper pilot, earliest in the morning.*

Your payment is transferred to your accounts and the 100 rupees note will be delivered to you before time."

Back in the laboratory, LSD and Dr. Batra carried out the placement of all the wires and kept talking to each other while doing so.

Abhilash, meanwhile, helped Shahista in preparing a list of questions to put up.

"You must start from Sushen, one of his own names he had revealed." Abhilash suggested.

"Why Sushen specifically? Why not any other name?" Shahista was perplexed.

"Because, that is in my view, the oldest of all and happens to be one end of this tangled thread. The other being Om Shastri. Or, you could begin by asking all he knows about the Satyug."

"I am a bit confused. Who was Sushen?" Shahista said in an apologetic yet demanding tone.

"Alright! During Ramayana, which is Treta yuga, the second after Satya yuga, in the war between lord Ram and Rawan, Lakhman (lord Ram's younger brother) was hit by a deadly arrow by Indrajeet (Rawan's son). It is said that only one herb had the ability to save Lakshman's life called Sanjivni buti at mount Dunagiri in Himalayas. The vaidya (doctor) who suggested the sanjivni buti was known to be Sushen. You must have seen the epic picture of Lord Hanuman flying with a mountain in his left hand. If he is talking of Vidur, it's in the Mahabharata, that is, the Dwaparyuga. And that means, Sushen must be as known as Sushen from the legendry Ramayana who, according to the stories, saved the life of Lakshman

by suggesting Sanjivni buti herb, for which Lord Hanuman lifted the whole mountain.", Abhilash explained.

"So, you want to say that in order to sort out the connections between all the names, we need to begin from Sushen, that is, the Treta yuga?", Shahista cleared the clouds of doubt from her head.

"I did what you asked me to, and I've stumbled onto something" L.S.D said.

"What?" Abhilash was curious.

"Vidur is said to be Dhritrashtra's brother, the most knowledgeable and wise person of his era."

"and Sanjay?"

"Sanjay was Dhritrashtra's advisor and also worked as his eyes to the world. His father was Gavalgan."

"So, I was right!" the usual self of Abhilash beamed with pride. And LSD added even more to it by confessing, *"Hmm! Looks like you were!"*

"Exactly, you see, it sounds crazy, but I'm serious. There is surely some association between this man and the man from Tretayuga. And, it's odd that all our answers lie with only one person, Om Shastri. So, we must start from there."

After hooking up Om to the lie detector, Dr. Batra curiously engrossed himself in his computer. Seeing this Dr. Shahista joined him leaving Abhilash. As Dr. Srinivasan entered the laboratory, Dr. Batra called out to him, *"Sir, we are ready!"*

"Proceed, then." replied Dr. Srinivasan, with a cold gaze.

Shahista requested, *"Om, please cooperate. I assure you that you won't be harmed."*

Om nodded half-heartedly. Dr. Tej and LSD did the needful. They connected Om with various wires and cables.

Within a few minutes, Om found himself extensively tied. Cords ran from his head, chest, arms and feet, and diverged in two opposite directions. The ones that originated from his head were further connected to a computer, and a machine, which in turn was secured to a projector screen. All others ran straight to the lie detector. Dr. Batra and LSD were done with their part of the preparation.

Shahista had readied her questions with Abhilash's help. Everyone was set to start; all the lights were switched off. Darkness swept in. The only light that existed came from the computer screens. LSD pressed some keys on her system and finally hit enter. As soon as she did that, a sheet of paper was scratched by some pins, sketching a graph. Some images appeared on the screen for a split second and went off. Om had opened his eyes.

The screen won't show any images when Om's eyes were open. As he blinked, the brightness in the room increased. Screen projected the time of the day, the places, the attire of the people that were being projected, seasons, cultures; everything flew past all of them without making any sense.

The guards in the room were alert and loaded their guns for any unwanted activity. The faces in the room were also being displayed in a jumbled form as Om's thoughts kept on skipping rapidly. Shahista realized that Om's thoughts needed to be controlled. For which, she had to give Om a feeling of calmness and safety.

To do that, Shahista held Om's shoulder, and said, *"Om, its okay. Calm down. You are not alone. Open your eyes and look at me. Take deep breaths, let loose your body, relax, de-stress yourself."* in a soothing voice.

As Shahista spoke, the screen changed gradually and things got visible even more clearly. The images stood still a while before moving out of the queue.

Dr. Srinivasan ordered the guards to be alert.

As his voice registered on Om's eardrums, Dr. Srinivasan could see himself on the screen. Following that, the landscape of a village flowed in. Flowing water, greenery everywhere, came into view. Dr. Srinivasan's gaze deepened and he grew serious. Thereafter, came the image of a government school, some children sitting on old worn-out wooden benches, and a few English men in the uniform of the East India Company. The image seemed prior to India's independence. This image was a jolt out of the blue for Dr. Srinivasan, who was shaken to the core.

Everyone except Shahista had clearly noticed that change in expression and the uncomfortable body language.

Shahista said, *"Om, are you ready to do this?"* And as she said that, the screen turned blank.

"Yes!" came the answer from Om Shastri.

The lie detector beeped, which meant Om wasn't really ready.

All the eyes turned towards the direction of the beep. Om's too. He then looked at Shahista, who had a slight trace of a smile on her face. Shahista spoke maturely, *"It's okay. I understand. But we have to start this now. Om, when you open your eyes, we lose the visuals. So, you have to keep them close while speaking."* she explained.

Om silently closed his eyes. Shahista looked towards Dr. Srinivasan first, and then towards Dr. Batra. Both bowed slowly. She took a deep breath that stabled her heartbeats, closed her eyes for a moment and started the procedure.

"Who is Sushen?" Shahista asked her first question.

Om was silent for a while, but he knew his memories would say it all, and so he spoke.

"It was me."

As he said that, the picture of a village and a forest flashed on the screen. Tribal people could be seen, donned in less but clean clothes, bare footed, carrying bows and arrows. Numerous trees and flowers could be seen. It seemed to be a rich and fertile land, with mountains, amazing species of plants and flowers, and dense forests with high falls.

"What is this place?" Shahista questioned.

"A village in Southern India.", replied Om.

"Who were you there?"

"I worked as a Vaidya (a person who makes herbal medicines and cures the diseases of common people) there. People approached me for various treatments. I knew of every root, bark, leaf and flower that ever grew on the mountain. I knew of each disease and its cure." Om said.

"Where exactly is this village?" Shahista tried to dig out some more data.

"It now falls under the Kanyakumari." He informed.

"Whose lives did you save?"

"I saved many lives. One of them was Laxman. I also served many people and monkeys during the war." came the revelation.

"You mean, the Laxman from the Ramayana?" Shahista confirmed.

"Yes."

"How is this possible? How are you alive even today?" Shahista had decided she won't lose her mind now and would concentrate on her work.

"I didn't age since then. I feel tired at times, but without any food or rest, I get energized automatically. I fall ill sometimes, but right before death can engulf me, I start recovering again. I don't die." he disclosed.

The silence in the room became uncomfortable and the atmosphere turned somber.

Shahista got hold of her and said, *"How did you look at that time?"*

Om started thinking and as he did that, a man materialized on the screen. Long beard, saffron colored clothes and *lungi* (an Indian outfit that was worn by ancient men), wooden footwear, and a turban on the head. His surroundings were essentially plants and herbs, with a few unusual utensils and lotions in front of him and herbs diluted in water. The man had just the resemblance of Om Shastri. The same face, the same man he was today. He also flipped images of Chanakya and Ashwathama.

All of a sudden, Dr. Batra stood up from his seat and screamed, *"This is bullshit! No! This is unacceptable!"*

As he thundered in rage, he started walking towards the door.

Om opened his eyes, and the room went dark. One of the guards switched on the light.

Dr. Srinivasan and Shahista rushed to stop Dr. Batra and blocked his way.

Dr. Batra echoed, *"Sir, we are dealing with a mental patient here! I can't take all this anymore. He is building up fantasies here!"*

"Why is the lie detector not beeping then?" Dr. Srinivasan debated.

"Because his pulse is normal. When someone tells a lie, their blood pressure fluctuates and their heartbeat rate shoots up. Our machine notices such changes and notifies us accordingly", Dr. Batra answered with reason.

"And these images we are seeing?" Dr. Srinivasan continued.

"*The images we are seeing are those created by his imagination, which, he thinks, are real. He is obsessed with his stories and thoughts and this obsession has led him to believe that he was actually a part of all that he says. He reads his own fantasies like he has lived them.*" Dr. Batra reasoned.

"*Imaginations are blurred, Tej. They can never be as clear as we are witnessing right now. Only real incidents and people can be clearly traced in our thoughts.*" Shrinivasan replied in anger.

"*Right and this man thinks very strongly that all this is real. So, he never perceives anything like an imagination. He believes he was present then, and that he lived it all.*" Dr. Batra grew even more adamant with his view of the situation.

"*Sir, it is vividly described in all the Hindu mythological books, the Ramayana and all others. And he has studied those books so deeply that he thinks he actually belongs in it. He never realizes that he is lying. He is diseased, sir. It's an abnormality. Cases like his are numerous across the globe.*" Dr. Batra asserted.

"*The session needs to end here!*" Dr. Srinivasan said, checking his watch.

"*Let us continue tomorrow. For now, assemble for the dinner, and he walked away*".

Within no time the interrogation room was empty. The security took Om to a secret place. He was handcuffed and was surrounded by the guards.

Later everybody started discussing about the day. As they were done with the dinner, Dr. Batra suddenly asked, "*Abhilash, it's interesting to hear all these tales from you, and you recite them well. They are adding to my knowledge and might help me in the interrogation, too."*

"Thank you. This is what I have been called here for, I suppose." Abhilash replied rather humbly.

"Tell me about Ashwatthama." asked Dr Batra.

Abhilash answered, *Dronacharya was the royal preceptor to the Kauravas (the 100 brothers) and Pandavas (the five brothers). He was a master of advanced military arts, including the divine weapons or Divya Astras. Arjuna was his favorite student.*

Learning that Parasurama was giving away his possessions to brahmanas, Drona approached him. Unfortunately, Parasuram only had his weaponries left. He offered to give Drona the weapons as well as the knowledge of how to use them. Thus, Drona obtained all of his weapons, and his title of 'acharya' and called Dronacharya.

"Abhilash I asked you about Ashwatama Not some Dronacharya." said Dr Batra irritatedly, to which Abhilash replied *"Sir it is important to know about Dronacharya to understand Who Ashwthama is. Dronacharya did many years of severe penance to please Lord Shiva in order to obtain a son who possessed the same valiance as Lord Shiva himself and so came Drauni also called Ashwathama."*

"Ashwathama is one of the seven immortals. He is believed to be the lone survivor who actually is still alive, who actually fought in the Kurukshetra war.

He was born with a gem on his forehead which gave him power over all other living beings lower than the humans. In fortitude, he was equal to a mountain, energy to fire. In gravity, he was equal to an ocean, and in wrath, to the poison of the snake.

The gem protected him from attacks of ghosts, demons, poisonous insects, and animals. Dronacharya loved his son very much. Ashwatthama was a mighty fighter who fought against the Pandavas, on Kaurava's side. Ashwatthama had his mastery in the science of weapons and is regarded as the foremost amongst warriors.

Dronacharya and Ashwatthama were loyal to Hastinapur (the kingdom of Dhitrashtra, the father of the Kauravas). Ashwatthama's father Dronacharya was the best of all warriors. Lord Krishna knew that it was not possible to defeat Dronacharya when he had bow and arrow in his hands. Krishna also knew that Dronacharya loved his son Ashwatthama very dearly. So, Krishna suggested Yudhishthira and other Pandava brothers that, if he were convinced that his son was killed on the battlefield, then Dronacharya would be desolate and would disarm himself in grief.

Lord Krishna suggested that Bhima (one of the Pandavs) kill an elephant by name Ashwatthama and claim to Dronacharya that he has killed Dronacharya's son Ashwatthama. After killing the elephant as advised, Bhima loudly declared that he had killed Ashwatthama. Dronacharya however, did not believe Bhīma's words and approached Yudhishthira (The eldest among pandavas). Drona knew of Yudhishthira's firm devotion to truth and that he would never ever utter a lie. When Dronacharya approached Yudhishthira and questioned him as to whether his son was dead, Yudhishthira responded 'Ashwatthama is dead. But it is an elephant and not your son'. Krishna also knew that it was not possible for Yudhishthira to lie outright. On his instructions, the other warriors blew trumpets and conches, raising a joyous noise in such a way that Dronacharya only heard that "Ashwatthama was dead", but could not hear the latter part of Yudhishthira's reply.

Out of grief, and believing his son to be dead, Dronacharya descended from his chariot, laid down his arms and sat in meditation. Closing his eyes, his soul went to Heaven by astral travel in search of Ashwatthama's soul.

While he was defenseless, he was executed by the Pandavas. Thus, on the fifteenth day of the battle, Guru Dronacharya was killed by the cheating of Lord Krishna and the Pandava brothers. The incident took Ashwatthama aback, and so he decided to anyhow end the chapter of Pandavas.

On the last night of the war after Duryodhan's defeat (Duryodhan was the eldest of the Kauravas, the hundred brothers) the very disturbed and restless Ashwatthama was sitting sleepless under a large tree.

An owl, bushing a group of crows, caught his attention. This gave him an idea of attacking the Pandavas camp at night. With a few surviving warriors, he attacked the camp on the eighteenth night of the war.

Ashwatthama burned the entire Pandava camp to ashes, leaving nothing behind. He moved on and killed many prominent warriors of their army, too.

He also killed Pandavas' all five sons, Upa-pandavas, while they were asleep, believing them to be the five Pandava brothers. In some versions of the story, he knew that they weren't the Pandavas, but killed them anyway, because he couldn't find their father. Ashwatthama believed that it was acceptable for him to attack the unexpected Pandavas, due to his father's death by unjust means; although he did believe his vengeance to be justified, he was warned by people of his own side that it was not.

When Pandavas returned to the camp with Lord Krishna after the night, incensed over this act of Ashwatthama, Lord Krishna cursed him with immortality, and deceased life till the end of Kaliyuga, and took the gem of Ashwatthama's forehead saying, "This wound will never heal!" This was the story of Ashwatthama." Abhilash concluded. *"Let us move towards our sleeping area now"*, LSD proposed.

She popped out of her seat immediately.

All others left their seats along, and walked behind Abhilash guided by guards.

8 - CRYPTIC CHEST

It was a windy night, while walking through the dark lobby, the only source of light was of the swinging lamp at the end of the corridor.

LSD waved Dr. Shahista and removed her laces as soon as she entered the room, her room was huge, but it had damp smell though it was nicely decorated with ancient lamps and furniture, seemed it wasn't used for a very long time.

In the next room, Dr. Shahista was worried about her children, she sat on her chair and reclined looking at the ceiling, while others were still settling in their rooms.

Dr.Shahistas eyes were heavy and drowsy, and soon she fell asleep.Late night Dr Shahista got up in a rush as she saw a shadow outside the door, and felt somebody is walking outside her room. She quickly got off the chair and opened the door to check outside. Dr Shahista walked till the end of the dark corridor and realized there was no body. All she heard was the cluttering sound of the waves. She turned back suddenly, and found LSD standing there. Dr. Shahista screamed in fear. *"What are you doing here?"*

LSD gasped, *"I was scared alone, I want to stay with you. Can I sleep in your room, please?"*

Dr Shahista nodded in acceptance, wiping her sweat off.

They both entered Dr. Shahista's room. LSD threw her bag on the couch and started unpacking her bag.

Dr Shahista asked,*" Did you hear someone walking around?"*

LSD replied with fear, *"yes I saw somebody's shadow outside my window, but it was dark and I had my headphones on so I couldn't hear a thing. I am glad I couldn't."*

She giggled, *"I don't want to see or hear a ghost. I am not comfortable at these old places, they are always haunted."*

Dr. Shahista put her glass of water back and comforted LSD by contradicting her and says, *"There is no such thing as ghosts."*

Curious LSD asked, *"I don't understand, what were you doing outside?"*

Dr.Shahista gulps down the story about the haunting shadow, as LSD was already frightened, so she continued," *I am worried about my family and I want to speak to them, but its too late"*

LSD tried to console Dr. Shahista," *relax I am sure your family will be fine, and we will be out of this very soon."* crossing her fingers.

Dr. Shahista takes a deep breath and walks to her bed.

LSD puts her glasses back, opened her screen and interrupted the silence of the room as she clicked her laptop keys. Dr. Shahista fell asleep within no time.

Meanwhile, Veerbhadra has travelled to Port Blair (Capital of Andman and Nicobar) in the dark of the night with two of his men in a speed boat to receive the delivery of the chest. He receives the chest. A pair of eyes witnessed him from a distance handling the chest. Veerbhadra left back for Ross Island followed by the unknown.

The night passed.

Shahista's sleep broke with the knock at the door, and noticed an envelope in the room. She opens it and wakes up LSD. Envelope had details regarding their session's timing. It was bright outside.

Post breakfast Dr. Shahista and Dr Batra walked towards Dr. Shrinivasan's chamber, while others proceeded to the interrogation room.

Meanwhile, Veerbhadra also entered Dr. Shrinivasan's room, and looked around for Dr. Srinivasan. He walked towards him with two gunmen and two boxes in his hands. These were Om's lockers.

"Open it right here!" Dr. Srinivasan ordered Veerbhadra.

Dr Shahista and Dr. Tej Batra were there for some discussion so they also joined,

As the boxes opened before them, they were left astonished. The boxes contained notes written even before the history began shaping itself and being recorded. Kept on some faraway land, secured, the pages were scribbled mostly in Sanskrit, apart from some that were in Hindi and Prakrit (an amalgamation of Pali and Sanskrit).

They were not the pages that one saw today. They were copper sheets. Each sheet had a name engraved on it as a header. They were the names Om had claimed to be his.

An old *Kharal* also emerged out of the box, apart from a few big, heavy finger rings, not to be seen or used today.

Old and rare coins, used for trade by different rulers and even more scripts jotted down in the Devanagiri hand and even Urdu, surfaced.

"Sir, there's a piece of information I found in the locker. I personally secured it so as to hand it over to you directly." Veerbhadra interrupted.

"It's a map, sir, with some piece of metal, mercury bottle and a book."

The book was wrapped in leaves and a white cloth with blood stains on it. The book had a metal cover, and something carved over it.

Dr. Batra kept fumbling with the pages, as if he was searching for something. He turned and looked towards Dr. Srinivasan, who stretched his hands forward as a signal. Dr. wanted to linger over the pages a while, but he handed over the book to Dr. Srinivasan.

"Shall we proceed? If you are done?" Dr. Srinivasan said.

Dr. Srinivasan looked at the metal block and the map, and said, *"Yes. It's a map but map of what and which kind?"*

"The answer is right here sitting inside the room. Let's ask him directly." Shahista suggested.

"No, not now. Don't let him know that we already have it in our custody. First, complete the list of questions you have prepared." Dr. Srinivasan commanded.

"Okay, sir." Shahista replied.

"Send LSD to me. Veerbhadra, you be with them. Shahista, don't start until I come back." Dr. Srinivasan said.

They departed, nodding, as Dr. Srinivasan waited for LSD.

Dr. Batra almost ran and entered the room. He looked at Om reflecting both anger and confusion, went back to his seat and started working on the computer. Shahista walked over to Dr. Batra and found him very worked up. He was curiously searching for something in his computer.

"Tej, what are you doing?" she asked, concerned.

Dr. Batra kept working and didn't even look up from his screen.

"Are you okay? See, all of us are equally shocked and surpr...."

"Shh..." Dr. Batra showed a hand signaling Shahista to stay silent and kept doing his work.

Shahista felt offended, but stood by his side for a few seconds and then turned around to leave. Dr. Batra called her back.

"Shahista!"

She turned back and came, her eyes affixed on the screen.

"See this." Dr. Batra shifted the monitor in her direction.

"What is this?"

Dr. Batra started explaining it to her.

"Every cell in our body has tiny engines called mitochondria. They provide us with the energy we need. When these engines go down, our body starts ageing and decaying."

"What is the point, Tej?"

"The point is, if these mitochondria's start rejuvenating, the body may live longer than an average human." Dr. Batra went on.

"So, you want to say that these tiny engines never went down in Om's body?" Dr. Shahista tried to clear her head.

Tej tried explaining the other way round.

"The scientists today have formulated a way to extend the life time of yeast, which normally happens to be 6 days, to about 10 weeks. A tenfold increase, that is."

"And, how is that related to our concern?" Shahista was perplexed.

"*Shahista, those 10 weeks are analogous to 800 years of a human life. When two genes, RAS 2 and SCH 9 were removed from its DNA, the yeast's longevity came as a consequence. The same genes when removed from a mouse doubled its life span too!*" Dr. Tej continued.

"*So?*" questioned Dr Shahista

"*Sixty different genes responsible for aging the human body have already been discovered. My concern is that science has still a long way to go before claiming that it can do the same with us. And, my concern is contradictory to Om's claim.*"

"*You still think of him to be deceptive?*" Shahista asked, and then said after a short pause, "*See, Tej, I have a lot of reasons not to trust him, but a hell of a lot of reasons not to question his credibility, too.*

"*I need a sample of his blood.*" Dr. Tej said with determination.

Shahista slowly nodded her head, "*Dr. Srinivasan would never allow you to do that.*"

Meanwhile, Dr. Srinivasan was talking to LSD in his cabin

He laid a map in front of her and asked, "*Can you prove it to me that you are indeed the best? You have 06 hours to solve this puzzle, which is, to find out, the place in the map and where the spot leads us to.*"

LSD loved challenges and accepted all with open arms, as they allowed her to test her boundaries, to improve her and to make her even more proud of herself. Her eyes beamed with excitement. She took the map from Dr. Srinivasan, and she turned around to walk out, Dr. Srinivasan said in a rather hushed voice, *"Keep this between us, LSD. Do not utter a word to anyone else. Your time starts now!"*

After a while, Dr. Srinivasan entered the interrogation room again.

9 - YESTERYEAR'S NOW

The next day was now to begin. As everyone settled, Shahista started the interrogation again.

"What other roles have you been playing apart from Sushen in all these years?"

A rapid series of places and faces depicting various events flashed on the screen.

The person on the screen had donned different traditional dresses and places portrayed different centuries and eras. But the face of the man was never changing, not even slightly.

Om had screwed up his eyes as he remembered all of his life and reflected expressions of fear, uncertainty, happiness, calmness, excitement, surprise, guilt.

His eyes watered then, as something, not so pleasant, passed through his head. He opened his eyes then to reveal they had gone blood red. As he did so, the images went off the screen. He seemed hurt and terrified. When he realized all were looking at him, he controlled himself and felt calm instantly.

Although, he was more than distressed by the fact that his life was being watched like a motion picture by strangers, and the secret will soon be known to them.

Everyone in the room saw unidentifiable visuals on the screen, but could easily make out three faces. The first, beautiful and elegant, which was engraved in Om's memories, clearly was that of a lady. This face was the basis of all the hassle Om underwent. She could be often seen in distinct outfits, too.

One mark of contrast between the woman and Om was that he never ever appeared to be old, whereas, she was projected in every age- as a teenager, an adolescent, a mature lady and an old woman. The lady's lifeless body was projected as being in three different ages, accompanied by Om in three different attires. When she was seen as being dead for the third time, Om had opened his eyes that very moment.

The second face that appeared repeatedly was that of a man with a strong build, carrying a bow and numerous arrows, apart from some other ancient, massive weapons.

The third face was that of Ashwathama later changing to Netaji Subhash Chandra Bose.

All were astounded to see the events unfolding before them, except Shahista.

In her tenure of hypnotism, she had seen patients in an even higher degree of distress than Om. So, any of it, didn't come as a shock to her.

She kept one hand on Om's hand to console him.

"Om, who else have you been living as all these years, other than Sushen? Answer slowly, one after another. Take your time and keep calm."

Om looked at Shahista and then closed his eyes, before he started speaking again.

In the woods away from the facility, two eyes revealing themselves from a mask, were fixed upon something, like those of an eagle on its prey, and were waiting for an event to occur. The person was equipped with modern war weapons and hi-tech devices.

In a room remotely located, a pair of old eyes were staring on a white screen which showed the inside of the laboratory in the facility where the team and Om sat. The man held a *Rudraksha Mala* (a string made of Rudraksha beads) in his hands. He picked up a cellular phone and pressed the redial button, as his eyes were fixed on the screen. He waited several seconds and then saw Dr. Srinivasan pick up the phone, nod his head, and calmly say, *"Yes, sir".*

Back in the interrogation room, the screen showed a man, cap-a-pie adorned in gold, surrounded with servants and maids, in a palace. He had Om's face. The palace was royal and elite. Om mumbled continuously as the images flew by on the screen.

He was saying, *"I have experienced all the colors of life. I have been rich and famous, with people craving to serve me, greet me with honor. On the contrary, I have been in rags too"*.

The visuals now portrayed Om as shivering in the cold, with barely some clothes on his body. The infrastructure showed without a doubt that a time gap of a century existed between the two consequent scenarios.

I have been an aghori. (The aghoris are known to engage in post mortem rituals sometimes involving cannibalism. They are also known to meditate and perform in haunted houses.)

"I have been an emperor. I have been a slave". The pictures showing Om in all these roles flowed on the screen.

Thereafter, Om was seen alone in some woods, clueless and petrified.

"I have been frightened and solitary person. I have been a loved man. I have also been a brave and fierce warrior."

Now, Om could be seen with a baby, horrified and handicapped in his lap, and the same pretty lady beside him. The image stood still for what seemed like an eternity. Then, Om opened his eyes that had gone moist. A tear rolled down his cheek, undisturbed. The first person Om saw was Dr. Shahista, who was also moved, but said nothing.

Om calmed down and started again, more practically and less sensitively.

"*I have been Govindlal Yadav and Protim Das and B.C. Chakraborthy. I have been Venkata Raman Rao and later I lived as my own son with the name Madhukar Rao. I have lived as Gursheel Singh and S.P. Reddy. Adhiriyan is also one of my several identities.*" The screen had been blank as he said this.

Abhilash leaned in towards Shahista and said, "*Ask him more about Vishnu Gupta*".

Shahista looked at Dr. Srinivasan, and got a silent consent.

"*You took so many names, but we already have them with us. They are all over the government records. But there is one name you didn't mention- Vishnu Gupta.*", Shahista questioned.

A blurred image occupied the screen that got clearer every moment.

Om now being projected was a bald one with only the typical Brahmin pony tail. Lord Vihnu's sign, a "U", appeared on the man's forehead, who wore a simple white piece of stoll and *dhoti* (a traditional garment wore in the ancient times).

Om began saying, "*I was the chief advisor of Chandragupta Maurya. One of the most important members of his council, I was also a good friend to him. I advised him in his personal and political affairs, apart from the issues of our warfares. I was also known by the name 'Chanakya'*".

As Om uttered this, the snapshot on the screen got so clear and they realised that it was Chanakya himself without a second of doubt. Parimal was calculating something as Om spoke, and as they finished, he took a piece of paper, stood up and walked across the room to Dr. Batra. The heading on the page said- "The time gap between lives of Sushen and Chanakya and the period between Chanakya's era and the present day".

Dr. Batra, after pondering over it for a while, said, *"That is what I am saying, impossible, unbelievable!"* Then he stood up and took the page to Dr. Srinivasan.

Dr. Srinivasan had a close look at the paper on which was scribbled in a not-so-legible handwriting.

SUSHEN- AT **7292 B.C.**---CHANAKYA- AT **321 B.C.** A TIME LAPSE OF---**6971** YEARS.

CHANAKYA-AT **321 B.C.**—PRESENT DAY-2016 A TIME LAPSE OF----**2337** YEARS

SUSHEN-AT **7292 B.C.**---PRESENT DAY-2016 TOTAL TIME LAPSE--**9308** YEARS

He managed to comprehend it and stood up with a sigh, saying, *"Continue the interrogation. Do not wait for me."* looking in Shahista's direction.

Meanwhile, LSD was lost in digging out meaning from the map, with the help of her gadgets by locating and connecting the map and by the ancient codes possible by rotating it in all the directions. It was evident from her curiosity and expressions that she was just a shuffle away from decoding the place, the map depicted. This would be another real breakthrough for the team.

In the woods, the man took out a device from his bag, and split it into four portions. The four independent devices, after being set free on the land, rolled into four different directions and placed themselves near the four corners of a nearby building. The man then pressed a button on his tablet, and could see a 3D image of the building in his tablet. The image was obstructed by red dots moving here and there which were people. The man could now keep an eye on each person entering and leaving the establishment.

With the piece of paper stating just a part of Om's total life span, Dr. Srinivasan walked the corridor, confused and disoriented. He soon stood abreast with a glass heavy door and flashed his ID. The door slid open and let him in.

After a short while, he found himself in front of another door being guarded by a couple of guards. The door opened only after the ratina scan recognition of Dr Sriniwasan. The doors parted and let him in.

Inside the laboratory, Shahista was saying, *"Do you even realize the meaning of whatever you narrated? You are trying to convince us that you were alive...*", as she was interrupted by Om.

"*In Treta Yuga*"

"*And you were also alive in Chandragupta Maurya's reign?*"

"*In the Kalyuga... I am still alive, and I'm not trying to convince anyone of anything.*"

Shahista took a deep breath and replied peacefully, "*Om, all these years span to a total of 9,000 years. You want us to believe that you have been alive for the past seven milleniums?*

"*I am alive since the Satyuga, through the Tretayuga and Dwaparyuga and now I'm in front of you in the Kalyuga.*" Om replied with a heavenly grin.

Abhilash was keenly listening to Om all this time he interrupted, "*Who were you in the Dwaparyuga?*"

Om looked at him, and then back at Shahista before closing his eyes, and said, "*I had many names in the history, but one of them that belonged to the Dwaparyuga was Vidur.*"

The image on the screen provided the proof that Om's words were facts, simply stated. Om appeared in a rich outfit, embellished in golden ornaments that hung low on his chest, and a golden crown to add to his majesty.

He stood beside a seemingly blind man, who appeared to be the king, and a blindfolded woman, presumably the queen.

"*Vidur! The brother of king Dhritrashtra and the queen Gandhari!*" Abhilash exclaimed.

Shahista continued before Om could react to the remark.

"*Since when are you alive? Tell us all that you remember, and have been through.*"

Om took a deep breath, and Shahista sensed his helplessness in it. He knew he was trapped and couldn't do much about it. So, he started.

10 - OUTDATED DECIPHERED

Meanwhile Dr. Srinivasan had entered a place that was hidden on purpose. A room with glass walls carefully disguised. He had brought with him the book that they had found in Om's locker. And, he handed over the book to the old man. The old man's eyes beamed with excitement as he took the book and started turning its pages. But soon the happiness turned into fury. After a long silence, the man spoke in a trembling voice, *"Where is the other half of this book?"*

Dr. Srinivasan stood confused and scared. He had thought the book was complete, though in a language illegible to any of the members in the facility, and with weird diagrams, maps and plants, not easily understandable. Before he could say it all to the man, the man shouted in rage, almost screeching, *"I said where is the second half of this book?"*

Dr.Srinivasan, replied hurriedly, *"Sir, I don't know, sir. This is the only book we discovered from the lockers."* He was scared as hell.

The old man slowly twisted his fingers, and gestured to Dr. Srinivasan to come closer to him. Dr. Srinivasan obeyed and kneeled down on the floor near the man's worn-out chair.

The old man grabbed Srinivasan by his hair, looked in his eyes gorily, and said, *"Look at this. Read this, you illiterate. Every alternate page in this book is missing."* he said shoving the book in Dr. Srinivasan's face, *"All the even numbered pages are intact here and all the odd numbered pages lie in the second book. This is a trick, so that the books are useless without each other. Where is the other book, now?"*

Dr. Srinivasan could see no page numbers, but surrendered quickly, saying, *"This is all we could get, sir. Dr. Batra understood this book as soon as he looked at it."*

The old man replied, disgusted, *"He understood things by looking at the diagrams of D.N.A and the extraction of genes from it.*

He can comprehend things but cannot conclude anything with this damned book even if he manages to read and understand the language. No one can come to a result with this book, because it is not complete. What else did you get from the lockers?"

"Sir, everything we found was sent to your personal laboratory, except a map which I handed over to LSD in order to decrypt." Dr. Srinivasan said with a dry throat.

At the mere mention of a map, the old man's eyes glittered.

"Map? That map is the key to the other book. How long will she take to decode it?" he asked rudely.

"I do not know, sir"

"Then ask her and tell me right away."

"Sure sir."

Dr. Srinivasan left the room in haste, feeling insulted and terrified.

Far off in the woods, another man, his face similarly masked, joined the first one, with an ancient key in his hand. They were about to raid the building they were keeping a close eye on. Both set their watches with the exact time and one of them showed another the internals of the building, moving red dots, and signaled at the entrance that they had to ambush in order to break into the building. They decided how many people each will take down before meeting at the common point, a door in the building without speaking at all.

Back in the interrogation room, just as Om was about to answer Shahista's question, LSD shrieked, *"YES!"*, as she shot both her hands up in the air, as if declaring herself the winner of some unannounced marathon. The guards, out of shock, turned their guns in her direction, on alert. All the heads turned towards her and Dr. Srinivasan entered the room. LSD looked around and realized what she has done! When she looked at Dr. Srinivasan, her expression changed. Suddenly, she did not feel like a winner, but a little girl who has broken her mother's faviourite vase. She looked at Dr Sriniwasan terrified and apologetic at the same time. She was so scared that tears welled up in her eyes.

Shahista stood up to console her but Dr. Srinivasan stopped her from doing so.

He walked up to LSD and took her hand to take her out of the room.

When they crossed the door, he asked,

"Why did you scream?"

"Because, I deciphered the map you gave me, sir".

"Good. I was coming to you for the same. Where is it?"

"Sir, actually, in the map, they intentionally exchanged the latitude and longitude values of the location. The degrees and the decimals above that were interchanged; the water bodies were converted to landscapes and vice versa, so that the location couldn't be easily deferred."

"LSD, I am least interested in this. Just tell me the location." Dr. Srinivasan said rather impatiently.

LSD rushed inside the room again, jotted down something on a piece of paper from her screen, and came back within a minute.

She handed over the slip to Dr. Srinivasan, and said, *"These are a series of mountains, woods, and caves in Sri Lanka and this is the exact location in the map."* she pointed out to a spot. *"It's an old cave like structure"*

"Okay, go back inside." was all Dr. Srinivasan said.

LSD didn't get her part of the much deserved appreciation for the great job she had done. But she was a self motivated girl and praises din't matter much to her.

She nodded silently, said under her breath, *"Okay, sir"*, and walked back into the room.

Dr. Srinivasan took a sigh of relief with the paper in his hand, and rushed to the secure vault of the old man.

Om Shastri continued with his answer in the lab.

"One day, I opened my eyes in a hut with three old rishis (Brahmins who pray and preach spirituality). The hut was big and crowded with followers from outside. I saw them from the holes of the mud walls. One of the rishis came to me and said," "How are you feeling, son?""

As Om narrated the incident, the picture started playing on the screen, wherein, a fair and tall man, above fifty years of age, stood smiling. He was wearing a plain, white *kurta,* and a *dhoti,* with a pair of wooden slippers. Red and yellowish threads circumvented his right wrist, while a white thread ran from his left shoulder to his right waist and back again.

I can never fail to recall them and the first flashes with them, as they are the first people I saw in life.

"I am feeling hungry, sir. Where am I?"

"Before you ask where you are, you must ask who you are" "the rishi replied with a smile."

"I wanted to tell them who I was, but I then realized that I didn't know it myself." Om confessed.

"Who am I?" "the man asked."

"So that is why you said that you don't know your real name when we asked you about it?"

Abhilash intervened and had to bear the stares of Shahista and Dr Batra for disturbing Om in between. Abhilash read their looks and immediately understood that he had to remain silent. Om continued, and the screen too followed him.

"As the rishi entered the room, the other three touched his feet and bowed in front of him with reverence. The revered rishi sat beside me and put his hand on my head."

"Why don't I remember anything?" "I asked."

"Because you don't need to; you are forty years old. Consider today as your first day in this world. You need rest now as you have many wounds in your body, some freshly stitched. So, don't exert yourself." "The rishi said."

"I was lying on the bed and still could see scars and stitches on my hands and chest."

"I am hungry", "I said."

"I know, son. But you can't be fed. You will have to stay hungry. Now, you must sleep." "rishi told me."

"One of the other rishis signaled something, he came immedietly with a liquid in an earthen flask. I gulped it down in haste as it was to quench my thirst. After a while, I fell asleep.

When I woke up, it was dark outside. I thought I had slept for a few hours, but later I was told that i had been in a deep slumber for 150 days, that is, nearly four months. It was raining when I had slept, which proved that they were right, because, when I woke up, I was chilled to the bones. I was still famished, and nothing in the hut had changed. All the three rishis still sat working by the fire, with herbs and solutions.

I found myself lying on a mat on the floor. My body was still embraced in stitches and cuts. The senior rishi entered the hut again and everyone bowed to him.

He accepted their greetings and looked at me. He came to sit next to me and handed a big vessel. Another Rishi came and poured water till it was full. I knew nothing as to what should be done with it.

He guided my face above the vessel and then, for the first time ever, I saw myself. I was full with cuts and stitches on my face. Even my head showed signs of a battle. I was almost bald with patches of hair here and there. I looked like a demon."

The visual of Om on screen was so disturbing that Dr Shahista and LSD had to look away. Nothing on his face looked normal, every feature was deformed.

"How do you feel, son?" "the rishi asked me."

"Who are you?" "I countered."

"I am Devodas, also known by the name of Dhanvantri. You can call me Kasiraja. That is what they all call me. Now, tell me, how you are feeling?"

"Kasiraja replied with an amiable smile."

"I am hungry", "I repeated."

"I know, but there are two more full moons to go before you can eat anything solid. Till then, you must learn to endure the hunger. You must take only the potions that the sages prepare." kasiraja replied."

"How will I subsist? I will die!" "I argued."

"You will get through as you have done so since the last four months. As a matter of fact, if you eat something, you will surely die. Now, you must rest." "said the humble rishi."

"Kasiraja took the mirror and walked till the door to leave the hut, when I asked," "Tell me who am I? What is my real name?"

"He turned back and said," "You didn't have a name in the past. At present, you will go by the name Mrityunjay, and will have many names in the future."

"Kasiraja then left the hut and called out," "Sushruta!"

"One of the three sages in the hut was Sushruta. Sushruta stood up and called out," "Ji Gurudev!" "and left the hut, too."

"After a while, Sushruta came back with a flask in his hands. He came and handed it over to me. The solution smelt like mint and was green in color. I was ravenous to resist anything edible. So, I consumed it in a single sip. Sushruta watched me with pity in his eyes and a smile on his face. He was older than me. After a few days, he told me that he was 49 years old. Dhanvantri was almost 70 years old.

After I drank whatever it was, Sushruta took it from me, and said," "I am Sushruta, one of the ten sages Kasiraja has selected to impart the knowledge of Ayurveda. We are the first three descendants of Kasiraja. Right now, we are residing in the Himalyan Ranges. He is Devdrath and that is Nagendra."

Most of the people present inside the lab were unaware of the names. But, Dr. Shahista and Dr. Batra recognized them, being in the field of medical science. Om continued.

"When Sushruta was talking to me, Devdrath came in carrying a bundle of banana leaves and handed them over to Sushruta. I didn't speak a word and just heard their conversation."

"Mrityunjay, I have to size all your scars on these leaves, so that we may perform the surgery and remove them from your body", "Devdrath spoke."

"He took the measures and prepared some Ayurvedic medicine and herbal solutions and applied them to my wounds. Soon, I started recovering. I got well acquainted with them as I shared the hut with them for months, Sushruta, Nagendra, Devdrath, and me.

As time passed, I started helping them in their daily chores and learnt from them. I knew nothing about myself and the world and so I started learning everything I could amongst them. While helping them, I gained knowledge about Ayurvedic system of medicine.

Sushruta was the first descendant of Dhanvantri. Apart from practicing medical science he was given a very crucial task. The assignment was to compile the teachings of Guru Dhanvantri, add more to it by his own experience and build a series of books, which in today's world is known as…" "Sushruta Samhita!" exclaimed Dr. Batra from behind Om. Om paid no heed and went on.

"Sushruta Samhita is an important classic Sanskrit text on surgeries by Sushruta, and is of the three foundational texts of Ayurveda. It is divided in two parts- Purva Tantra, and Uttar Tantra in 184 chapters containing the description of 1120 ailments, 64 preparations from mineral resources and 57 preparations based on animal sources."

Parimal whispered to Dr. Batra, *"Sir, how do you know Suss...Sushmita?? Or whatever na.....me you uttered? A.....nd who are Sus....hruta and Kasiraja and Dha..nvantri?"*

"The word is Sushruta Samhita. Sushruta is regarded as "Founding Father of Surgery". He was the first person to devise and practice plastic surgery." Dr. Batra replied in a hushed voice.

"Suu...shruta Samhita! And what about Dha..nvantri and Kasiraja?" Parimal asked innocently.

"Kasiraja, Devodas and Guru Dhanvantri are all the names of one person. Dhanvantri is believed to be the God of Ayurvedic treatments." Abhilash elaborated.

"It is said that he reappeared as Devodas, "The Prince of Banaras" and is also known as Kasiraja", LSD joined in the conversation.

Abhilash carried on, saying, *"Dhanvantari relieved the other Gods of old age, diseases, and death, too. He enlightened ten sages with the skill of surgery on his Himalyan retreat. Sushruta was considered by Dhanvantari as his best prodigy and also taught other divisions of Ayurveda.*

Dhanvantari is regarded as the almighty of all the branches of medicines. There is a voluminous glossary and medical science's material in a section known as the "Dhanvantari Nighantu", the most ancient text available in its field.

We worship Dhanvantari for good health, especially on the occasion of Dhanteras (one of the days that is counted as part of the festival of Diwali in Hinduism), which is considered as the birthday of Dhanvantari." Abhilash imparted.

Back in the old man's room, Dr. Srinivasan took a sigh of relief whilst handing over the map and the piece of paper, with the location jotted on it, to the old man, who praised Dr. Srinivasan for the rapid results. Dr. Srinivasan hadn't recovered from the trauma he had experienced when he last came into this room.

The old man, being thoroughly absorbed into the enthusiasm of the accomplishment, didn't take notice of Dr. Srinivasan's gloom, and moreover, ordered him the same. The new task for Dr. Srinivasan was to send Veerbhadra to the location marked on the map and bring what ever he finds straight to him. Dr. Srinivasan silently collected the map from the old man and left the room.

After a while, the masked men in the woods saw Veerbhadra walking out of the facility. The three-dimensional view on their screens showed the facility where Om was kept a hostage. The location where Veerbhadra was heading to was in Sri Lanka. Ross Island, being the extreme south of India, wasn't very far from the spot. Veerbhadra ordered one of the guards to arrange a private chopper, because he was given the least time to finish this job.

The men saw a map clutched in Veerbhadra's hand and gussed the development instantly. They were compelled to alter their plans. They now decided that one of them would follow Veerbhadra and the other would keep an eye on the happenings in the building.

One of them gave a part of his weapon to the other and left to follow Veerbhadra. The chopper in the air was being shadowed by an advanced speed boat on the waters below.

The discussion between Parimal and Abhilash stopped midway as Dr. Srinivasan returned to the interrogation room. As he entered, his image flashed on the screen, which proved that Om recognized his presence with closed eyes.

As Dr. Srinivasan saw his image, he babbled with irritation, *"Why am I on the screen? What is going on here? Why don't you guys do sincerely what you have been called for, and return to your respective homes?"* he thundered.

His behaviour was unexpected and left everyone stunned. Dr. Shahista and Dr. Tej got closer to him to ensure he was alright, but Dr. Srinivasan didn't entertain them and sent them back with a swift movement of his hand.

Om was staring with a wild expression at Dr. Srinivasan, and closed his eyes again as he saw Shahista walking back towards him. Shahista sat and signaled Om to go on.

11 - MRIT-SANJEEVNI

"It took more than a year to compile the Sushruta samhita. Every day, without failing, Sushruta dictated and Nagendra wrote it all for hours together starting early morning. Devdrath assisted them with everything they needed, along with nursing me as I had undergone a lot of surgeries all through my body. Those were plastic surgeries, as you all know it today, so I needed a lot of care and attention.

After I recovered, I helped Devdrath, apart from listening to Sushruta and Nagendra. Kasiraja often visited us to make sure I was recovering and to keep track of the progress of the book.

As time passed, I became a part of the place. I was living a peaceful life. All my scars vanished gradually. There was something that troubled me. Each night, Sushruta went to Kasiraja's hut for quite some time and the time when no one else was allowed to enter it."

"So, one day I asked Devdrath," "Why Sushruta goes to Guruji's hut every night?"

"Devdrath replied with equal incorruptibility," "I wonder the same. Moreover, I asked him once, but he refused to tell me".

"Nagendra was attending to us, and so, replied," "He goes to take notes for Mrit Sanjeevani".

"Both of us looked at him and then Devdrath asked him," "If this is true, how do you know about it?"

"Nagendra replied," "I followed him many a times and have seen him writing the procedures of Mrit Snajeevani".

"What is Mrit Sanjeevani?" "I asked."

"Mrit Snajeevani is a miraculous procedure of bringing the dead back to life." "Devdrath told."

"But, they say that no one can do that? Only Gods hold the power of giving life?" "I had asked, childishly."

"Devdrath replied," "Kasiraja is a God himself and..." "And I'll be the next" "Nagendra interrupted".

"The good news is that, dreams will always be free of cost", "Devdrath said."

"Has Mrit Sanjeevani been practised? Or is just theoretical yet?" "I asked."

"Why do you think you are alive? We have seen you dead a year ago. If Mrit Sanjeevani had been a theory, you would have been reduced to ashes long ago." "Nagendra said with a harsh tone which appeared full of hatred. I had never felt comfortable around Nagendra, but this was no time to ponder over petty issues. I was jolted by the news I had just received. That I was a lab rat, an experiment, and the only successful one. That moment, I stopped feeling like a normal human being. A sense of inferiority bred in me."

"How did I die?" "I asked."

"I read Devdrath's face which revealed that he was not supposed to let it slip. It also showed anger towards Nagendra for bringing this up. But, being the weakest of the three sages, he didn't mouth his anger. Numerous questions had clouded my mind, and my relief lied with Devdrath."

"We don't know that. When we saw you first, you were dead." "Devdrath said, smashing my expectations."

"Where did you find me?"

"We don't know where you died but, yes, we know where you were born!" "He replied sarcastically."

"Tell me! Maybe, I get some answers there." "I was hopeful."

"In Dhanvantari's hut. There," "he pointed," "Where Sushruta is writing the procedure of 'How to make a second Mrityunjay'", "he burst laughing."

"For the first time, I had many feelings growing up in me, the negative ones specially."

"Devdrath tapped his hand on my shoulder, and said," "We are unaware of you, but Sushruta knows. Maybe, he will tell you when the time comes."

"I always obeyed him. In fact, I never had an urge to disobey them until this moment.

After a while, Sushruta returned to find Devdrath and Nagendra fast asleep. My questions haunted me and kept me from sleeping, so I was wide awake. I wanted to know about myself, my life, my death and everything else.

Sushruta saw me and realized that something was not right. He came and sat beside me and stroked my hair with his fingers. "why are you not asleep?" He asked out of concern.

"Who am I?"

"Sushruta comprehended within a moment as to what might have befallen while he was away. He handled the situation with diplomacy, saying," "You are Kasiraja's son. He gave your life back as a gift. You are my younger brother. That is all you must know for now. Tomorrow is a big day for all of us and you should sleep".

"What is Mrit Sanjeevani?" "I pushed."

"As the name hit his ears, he shot an angry glance in Nagendra's direction and then replied with a sigh," "That is how we saved you, Mrityunjay.

You do not need nutrition or water for survival now. You may have them but, they are not a necessity for you anymore, unlike us. You will not age now or ever, which is why you have been named as 'Mrityunjay', Mrityu (death), vijay (victory) the one who conquered over death. You are not only a complete human being, but a far more advanced than normal humans, a enlightened version of this mankind."

"I was dazed by this revelation. Sushruta understood my confusion and went on," "Okay, think of it this way. We are all bound to a time circle. Time that neither reverses nor rests. It is the ship in which every being navigates. Time is the driving force of every life. Each life present on this earth has a time line and an age. But, you, my brother, have fallen out of this circle. The Divinity of time can't see you. You are undetectable to its eyes. Time, in you, has been put to halt, my friend. For this moment, time sees me, and deducts a second from my life span. Time passes through me constantly, but is constant for you. Time sees me talking to somebody but it wonders whom am I talking to. Therefore, I will age continuously and will die someday.

But you won't. This is what Mrit Sanjeevani is. And you are blessed to be Mrityunjay.

This book is a boon, in the right hands, for those people who are able to distinguish between, who should walk upon the Earth forever, serving the mankind and who should be erased. On the contrary, this book is a curse when in the wrong hands, it's a treacherous weapon. That's why, it is being safeguarded by Shri Kasiraja, unlike the Sushruta Samhita, and its compilation is kept a secret for everyone except me, being his only confidant. I am revealing this to you, because our reason behind this hideout is resolved. The objective, which was completing Mrit Sanjeevani, has been achieved, and Gurudev will instruct us soon to pack our belongings, and move back to our respective capitals to serve the mankind with the knowledge we have obtained from Gurudev."

"What about the Mrit Sanjeevani? Where will I go now? And what will Kasiraja do next?" "I flooded the questions."

"Guruji hasn't informed me as yet. He will tell whatever we need to know, at the right time but I believe that guru ji will retain you with him, as you are his creation, his son."

"I had some more doubts to be cleared, but before I could clear my head, Sushruta continued," "It's too late to talk now. We must sleep. Tomorrow is an important day. Don't worry. We will have enough time to talk tommorow.

You have waited for so many months. I'm sure you can wait for a night more. Goodnight, Mrityunjay!" "Sushruta concluded the conversation leaving me waiting for the morning."

"While I was asleep, I heard a disturbance in the hut. I managed to open my eyes, and saw Devdrath and Nagendra leaving the hut.

It was dawn. I then heard Kasiraj order them to prepare a feast for everyone. After a while, Nagendra came back, and took with him some leaves from beneath his cot. I fell asleep again."

"When I woke up, Guruji directed everyone to gather outside his hut. He came out, and addressed us," "Sages, dear sons, I have bestowed upon you all the knowledge I could have. It is time for you all to go back to your cities, save and serve others of our kind. You are all the few to become the first of saviours and surgeons. You have been the best of apprentices, and so, I have ordered a feast for all of you before you depart. I would want to see each one of you here, again after a year, to gather new knowledge from my further research."

"Kasiraja seated the seven sages for the feast prepared by Devdrath and Nagendra, whom he ordered to serve the food. He then gestured Sushruta and me to follow him into his hut. We followed him to his hut."

"Sushruta, you are my obedient and favourite son. For everyone else, the job is done. But, for you, it has just begun." "Kasiraja said."

"Guruji, my place is at your feet. It would be my honor to follow your instructions. Please, go on."

"I have not trained you to stay here and serve me. Your real purpose is out there, to save and serve people. Your name will be written in golden letters in the field of medicine. Reach out to the needy and perform your duties. But, I have some more responsibilities to assign to you", "Gurudev replied with an amiable smile."

"Tell me, Guruji. I will do it with full faith and devotion."

"Take Mrityunjay and Mrit Sanjeevani along with you. Mrityunjay should learn the ways of the world. You are best suited to

teach him that. Keep him with you for the whole year before returning here again. And, look after him like your own son."

"Sushruta's eyes had filled with tears. Controlling his emotions, he replied,"

"Guruji, I wanted the same, but could not ask you. You have always understood everything without me saying it. I take his full responsibility from this day."

"Also, Sushruta, Mrit Sanjeevani would not be safe here. The word would soon spread that Mrit Sanjeevani has been written, and the evil forces will come to get it." "Kasiraja said, concerned."

"Guruji, this is a treasure to the world and is a result of your continuous research and untiring practice. How can I carry it with me? It doesn't belong to me", "Sushruta said anxiously."

"Kasiraja calmly said," "Nor does Mrityunjay, my son!. But, you are the keeper of both these invaluable godsends. They are safe in your hands, than in any of the immoral's."

"I just stood there, listening to them."

"As you order guruji. What do you want me to do with it?" "Sushrut gave in."

"Take an oath to keep this book safe until you hand it over to me. And, Mrityunjay will help you in that." "Kasiraja affirmed."

"Sushrut promised to keep the majestic book safer than his own life."

"I watched as Kasiraja hand over the Mrit Sanjeevani to Sushruta, and heard him say," "Now, you may leave, and enjoy the feast with the rest of your brothers".

"Guruji, there is a request I want to make before taking your leave", "Sushruta politely said." "Yes?"

"Guruji, Mrityunjay is very anxious. He wants to know about his past. This is the one thing I can't help him with. Please help him getting over it or he wouldn't become the person you want me to make of him."

"Kasiraja smiled and glanced towards me. He directed me to sit close to him. I acted in accordance."

"What do you want to know?" "He asked humbly."

"Who am I? Where am I from? How did I die? And, how did you find me?"

"I was interrupted by Nagendra who entered the hut, with three bowls of kheer (one of the oldest desserts of India prepared from milk, rice, and sugar) arranged in a tray."

"He said," "Sorry Guruji. This is my last day here, and I committed the mistake of entering without consent. I waited outside, but it was taking too long. Everyone, including Devdrath, had already feasted. So, I considered bringing it here for all of you, else it might have lost its fresh taste."

"He handed a bowl to each of us. I wished he left soon, so I took my bowl readily, as my answers awaited me."

"As I was about to have my first sip, Kasiraja interjected."

"No! Mrityunjay, don't! You have not eaten anything since long. Three hundred seventeen days, to be precise, dear. Nine more days are to pass before you can have food."

"I kept the bowl back into the tray, feeling a bit awkward. Kasiraja supped from his bowl. After taking in the first taste, he made a face and immediately understood the same thing in a split second and warned Sushrut not to have it. The kheer contained a poisonous herb. But, before they could react, Nagendra launched an attack on Sushruta. Sushruta was the only threat who could have retaliated. Dhanvantari was too old to fight, and I was witnessing such an act for the first time in my life.

A minute later I saw Sushruta bleeding. He was attacked by a knife, which he had defended by using his arms. Dhanvantari tried helping Sushruta and struggled to stop Nagendra, but it was in vain. Leaving Sushruta helpless and exhausted, Nagendra set upon Dhanvantari. Sushruta, without wasting a moment, ran up to the Mrit Sanjeevani books, wrapped them in a white piece of cloth, and handed them over to me. The white cloth by then absorbed Sushrut's blood on it. I was already jolted by whatever was happening then, and this gesture added to it. Sushruta shook me hard to bring me back to the reality, and held my terror stricken face in his hands and whispered."

"Mrityunjay! Run! Run as fast as you can and as far as you can get towards South. Wait for me down the hill for a day. If I don't turn up, proceed onwards. Protect this book more than your life. Don't let anyone know that you have it. Now

go, my brother. Go!" "Sushruta said in haste, out of breath."

"He turned on his heels then, and plunged over Nagendra to set Dhanvantari free. This was the last thing I saw. Then I ran like a child scared and lonely. I paused on my way, and it took me about 24 hours to reach my destination. I then waited for him a whole day, as Sushruta said. But, he didn't arrive. Instead of losing hope, I began imagining that Kasiraja and Sushruta were walking down the terrain. And they were taking time to reach me.

In this fantasy, I waited another day, and one more, and some more days. But they never appeared. When I had left Kasiraja's hut, I had seen all the other sages sleeping under the open sky. I wandered in the series of Himalaya Mountains for about a year. My state worsened with every passing day without anyone to care. I learned drinking water and eating leaves from the animals in the rivers and forests. I got sick and starved to death, and had many deaseases. I even ate poisonous herbs by fault and was attacked by wild creatures that consumed me to death but never died.

I learned the cycle of life seeing the births and deaths of beasts. I continued wandering and one day saw a village down a hill. I was frightened of mankind after seeing Nagendra's act of violence for the book and thought not to go any closer. I returned to the woods and mountains and traced myself back to where I started from.

A year had passed now, and as I reached the hill top again, I saw skeletons scattered all over the place. I then realized that the sages were not sleeping the day I ran but were dead long back. I cried like never before or after that. I sobbed for people I knew, who were my friends, my family, and my entire world. I felt like an orphan and ran from one remain to another, but I could not make out who's Devdrath's, Dhanvantari or Sushrut. I thought they might have escaped alive somehow, my heart consoled my brain.

I sat on my knees, face towards the sky, wondered where my creators are, and prayed for their well being...

12 - THE FIRST OUTBREAK

Veerbhadra had reached Srilanka as ordered and directed. His movements were being keenly followed by a disguised man. A Shrilankan guide was paid highly to escort Veerbhadra to the desired location. The guide also agreed to arrange for some ammunition for him if need. The voyage began with twelve men in total, except the one following all of them. The man called up his partner, who stayed in the woods, waiting for the right time to complete the task.

In the woods, he was fully prepared to launch the strike. He attended the phone, nodded a few times, and said yes. Then, he disconnected. He looked up towards the sun, and then at his watch, waiting for the particular time.

As Om spoke in the interrogation room, Dr. Srinivasan's phone rang. Everyone got disturbed by the volume of the ring. The caller ID displayed a name that couldn't have been ignored. So, he indicated them to continue, and left the room picking it up.

"Yes Veerbhadra!"

"Sir, we are a mile away from the location and the wheels can't go any further. We are on feet now. Expect my call as I reach there." Veerbhadra's voice echoed through the phone.

"Veerbhadra, you are the bravest and the best fighter I've ever known. Get me everything you get there, undamaged. It is a matter of life and death. Please, don't let me down."

"I will do my best, sir. But, it would be convenient if I could know what we are looking for."

After a short pause, Dr. Srinivasan replied, *"We don't know that. All the best"*, and hung up the phone.

He then went towards the chamber the old man resided in.

The old man was in his usual self, angry and sick. He sat facing the screen, watching Om and the team. Dr. Srinivasan told him about the call he had just attended to. The old man was least interested in Veerbhadra's progress; he just wanted to hear the result. The result for him was the second book. So he directly jumped on the right question. *"Did he find the book?"*

"No sir." said Dr Sriniwasan.

"So what are you here for?" asked the Old man.

That was discourteous but Dr Sriniwasan had no answer, so he stood silent.

Back in the interrogation room, Om continued, *"I was lost in my thoughts, and mourning for the loss of my people, when I found myself fenced by some shadows. I brought myself up on my legs, and realized that some men were hiding when I had arrived there. And, now, they were approaching me. I knew it, that the shadows were not waiting for me."*

Shahista, for once, interjected him, and said, *"In the mountains, if not for you, what were they looking out for?"*

In the woods at Ross, the man received another call from his partner informing him about the movement in Srilanka's caves. Veerbhadra had come out of the cave with a metallic chest. He called Dr Sriniwasan and informed him about the chest. Dr Sriniwasan from the other side ordered him to open it. Veerbhadra was now striving to open it. Both the sides went silent in anticipation of what lay inside it.

"What is it in the box?" the man from the woods whispered, waiting and so did Dr Srinivasan. His partner replied him the same as Om Shastri revealed to Shahista and Veerbhadra replied Dr. Srinivasan.

"THE BOOK"

Veerbhadra held in his hands the other half of Mrit Sanjeevani.

Dr Srinivasan shot a glance to the old man on hearing about a book. He had already known about the book when he had seen the map. The old man was busy cutting banana leaves the size of his scars, when Dr. Srinivasan reiterated Veerbhadra's findings to him.

"The Book", Dr. Srinivasan mouthed. The old man got distracted and looked towards him with some insane excitement hidden in his smile.

He showed signs of mental imbalance as he yelled, *"Bring me the book! Now! Hurry! How long will he take? Tell him not to stop for anything. Just bring me the book, right away!"*

The old man repeated the same statements over and over again.

Dr. Srinivasan was terrified and astounded at his unusual conduct. But, he complied, and ordered Veerbhadra what the old man had demanded of him. The old man had started murmuring to himself like someone who was mad. The phone got disconnected.

As soon as the man in the woods heard about the book, he got tensed and his voice became heavy. The lines on his forehead deepened. He closed his hands in a tight fist, took a deep breath, as if preparing himself for something, and said in a throaty voice over the phone,

"Do whatever it takes to bring the book in your possession. Don't hesitate in killing anyone if need be. Come back soon. We are running out of time."

Dr. Srinivasan's phone rang again, Veerbhadra, the caller ID revealed.

"Yes, Veer?" Dr. Srinivasan answered it.

"Sir, we have also found some equipment and apparatus objects out here. We have a big bow, a few arrows and their carrier, apart from a crown, a golden kamardhani (an ornament to be tied around the waist) some carved metallic weapons, a box full of ornaments and some gold coins. Also, we have found some equipments and apparatus like that used in a laboratory."

Dr Sriniwas after listening said, *"Bring as much you can, but Veer, the book in your hands is the priority."*

In the interrogation room, Shahista kept on going with her duty.

"What happened next?" She asked.

"It had been a year. I had been alone, stranded. I had no idea what food was. I wandered in the mountains, and it had become my home. And, after a year, I was back at the place where I was born. I was amongst my family, the sages. Only they didn't talk to me now. Dead people, they don't talk."

As he went on, the bits and pieces of his memory flashed on the screen, evidently showing the remains of the people as Om remembered it, and Om's condition by then.

"The shadows around me were close to me now and the faces more clearly visible. I was left with no will to live any longer. The men were armed, and I was ready to taste what death had to offer me. So, I paid no heed to them, and did what I wanted to. I cried my heart out, like an orphan does for his lost parents. I knew that my days were

numbered, and those people would take me far away, and kill me. All through the year, I had come out alone. I hadn't changed my clothes. I had no idea how the beard had to be cleaned.

My feet were cracked. My hair had grown long enough to hide my face. In this attire, I could have been mistaken for a madman in the mountains. I was ready to die, but they weren't to kill me. They hit me hard on my head, the world spun around me, and I fainted. Few hours later, when I regained consciousness, I realised I was being held a captive, tied with chains to a chair, soldiers all around me equipped with bows and arrows aimed at me.

The man I faced, appeared to be the one on whose commands, the arrows would rip through me. He had been waiting for me to wake up."

"You will not be given a second chance. Tell me what I ask, do you understand?" "The chief spoke in his hushed voice."

"I nodded."

"Who are you? Whom did the skeletons belong to? What were you doing there?"

"I told him my name that was all. I knew nothing as to how much should be revealed and how much should be held back. So, I chose to hold back everything, and said," "I don't know how I reached there or who those people were."

"I behaved like an insane due to lack of mannerisms and basic conduct in me. They couldn't suspect me for anything as I carried no luggage along. Within a few days, they were convinced that I was no more than a burden upon them, who had to be fed twice a day only for being useless. So, they now knew that it was in their best interest, either to kill me or to set me free."

The whole team present in the interrogation was watching it all on the screen as a movie, and was convinced that every word from Om is as true as their lives.

"One day, hence, the commander ordered one of his men to make me presentable as I was to be taken to their king. My beard was shaven and I was bathed properly, after which I was given a new pair of clothes to put on my new body. The king had given the verdict of setting me free, sensing no threat in my survival. As I dressed up and looked in a mirror, I recognized Mrityunjay for the first time in my life. But, my happiness faded as it dawned upon me that I was a full grown man, and was good for nothing. I was hollow inside, with no love, no hatred, no peace, no commotion, no noise, but silence. My existence and otherwise, would not affect anyone here. Surrounding me were merry faces, both young and old, tied together by the Almighty. What could be worse than dwelling alone in this world full of people, good or bad? Tears rolled down my eyes. I couldn't end my life because I was bound to a promise, which Sushruta had taken from me, that I would protect the book more than my life. Otherwise, I had no reason to live. That one promise and those books drove life in and out of my body. I kept learning the ways of the world slowly and stealthily. I fell ill a few times, of diseases that had no cure. But, I didn't die."

As Om revealed the fact, the images on the screen showed Om, fragile and dying. But, the breaths he took were strong and healthy.

"*There was a time when I was living with a noble man, working as his servant, in exchange of food and shelter. He also used to give me some of his old clothes occasionally. My job was to to take care of his children, play with them and do whatever they demanded of me. In addition I also performed other household tasks like laundering the clothes, running the errands etc. Whilst I played with the children, I too learnt a lot of things that they did, apart from elementary reading and writing.*

As time passed, I became family to them and vice versa. I was treated like the best of all the workers. But, this didn't last long."

Om took a short pause. All looked at him with the same question in their eyes, why!

"*What went wrong?*" Shahista pressed.

"*I wasn't ageing at all. It started bothering me, as everyone else was growing old with time.*"

The people in the room saw it all as clearly as it was grounded in Om's mind. The kids could be seen growing up. The head of the family had grown feeble, too. But Om never showed the slightest signs of any change.

Veerbhadra was looking at the book in his hands. It had worn out critically. Veerbhadra had no idea how it could be so important to anyone. Just as he was pondering over the thought, he got alarmed by the sound of a bullet leaving a gun, and some more in a series. He turned back only to see five of his men lying dead. They had lost their life before anyone could fathom the source of the bullets. Veerbhadra ordered four of his men to run in the direction from where the bullets seemed to have originated, and catch the shooter alive. The rest, along with Veerbhadra, ran in the opposite direction towards their vehicles, with the book. This book is crucial as hell, thought Veerbhadra.

The men, who ran in the direction of the shooter, knew not who they were just about to encounter. They only woke up to the truth, seconds before their deaths. One moment they realised that they stood no chance of beating their target, and the next moment life ran out of their bodies. The fighting skills their opponent possessed were unbeatable. He exploited the oldest of the skills of combat, and the now extinct art of fighting a war. Perhaps, the death of the four men had not proved to be completely useless. It had bought time for Veerbhadra to escape with the book.

The mission of the man had failed, but it wasn't over. As he killed those men, he knew exactly what would rectify it.

The man in the woods received a call from his partner in Srilanka. He answered it immediately, *"Is it done?"*

"Negative. He got away with the book. Be prepared."

"How long will you take?"

"Half an hour, less may be. I'm close behind them."

"Okay. I'm ready to engage. How many?"

"There are three heading towards the facility. Nine are dead."

Dr. Srinivasan was halfway to the interrogation room when his phone rang. It was Veerbhadra. He answered it, while turning back to reach the chamber, in a haste.

"Yes, Veer!" He was out of breath.

Veerbhadra was panting on the other side, terrified how the events had unfolded. He was smeared in blood. He managed to reply in a choked voice, *"Sir, someone attacked us. Many of our men have been shot dead. Sir, something more critical than we know is going on here."*

Dr. Srinivasan, too, was horrified at this revelation. He had never ever witnessed a murder, and had no idea how the situation must be handled. He doubled his strides towards the old man. He put Veerbhadra on a hold. As he reached the old man, he noticed that he had been sweating profusely. He babbled,

"Our men have been murdered there in Srilanka. Veerbhadra is on the call. What is going on here? What is the worth of that book that people are dying for it? And who could possibly be an enemy to us? What are you making us do? Answer me!" Dr. Srinivasan thundered.

The old man stood up, walked up to Dr. Srinivasan, and snatched the phone from him.

"Where is the book?" he asked.

"The book is with me."

"How long will you need to reach here?"

"Thirty minutes or so, who are you? Where is Dr Shriniwasan?"

The old man disconnected the phone without any further questions or concerns. He didn't bother about the loss of life that had taken place.

Dr. Srinivasan stood there, looking at the old man's wobbly legs defeating him. He looked from head to toe at the merciless creature that stood there, insanely behaving. Then did he realise for whom he had been standing through thick and thin.

The old man was now seated on his chair, collecting a few things. Dr. Srinivasan brought himself together, and approached the man, taking small steps. He grabbed the hand rest of his chair, and spun him around all of a sudden to make the old fellow face him.

He then demanded in a beastly voice, *"What have you put us into? If men have been murdered there, it can happen here too. I am freezing the interrogation and other work untill I get answers I need.*

Dr. Srinivasan's eyes had gone red with fury. The old man all of a sudden stood up, and grabbed Dr. Srinivasan by his biceps, only to push him eight feet back with one swift movement of his hand. Dr. Srinivasan hit the wall hard and winced in pain. The old man was far too strong and speedy for his age. Dr. Srinivasan had never imagined a physical assault could come his way via this fragile looking creature. The old man, for the first time, straightened his back and stood abreast with Dr. Srinivasan, staring him straight in the eye. His eyes were terrifyingly big, and he didn't blink even once. His pupils remarkably contracted and expanded as they had their gazes locked. Dr. Srinivasan stared in terror, and the old man in rage. Then, the old man spoke calmly, and politely.

"It is not your team. It's mine. I have paid each one of them, and you, too. I have had numerous servants in my life. Out of them, only those who never asked 'what' and 'why', have died natural deaths. You understand?" he warned.

Without waiting for an answer, he pointed towards the screen showing the interrogation room and the people in it.

"Look at them. See the calmness on their faces. The reason behind this serenity is that they don't know what they should not. So, they are just doing what they have been told to. They hope to go back to their homes to see their families, because they trust you. Now you have two choices. Either, all these people go back home with their unanswered questions, or, you take the answers from me, in exchange for their lives."

Dr. Srinivasan ran his eyes over all their faces. He realised some of them were younger than his own children. Tears welled up in his eyes, and, the old man got his answer. He started back towards his seat, stopped at a distance, half turned, and said, *"No more questions, huh?"*

Dr. Srinivasan stood speechless. He left the chamber at once, and turning round the corner of the hallway, wiped his tears and took deep breaths. He stood there for some time to calm down. Suddenly something struck him and he rushed to the interrogation room.

Back there, Om was speaking.

"The word about me had spread in all the directions, which soon made me the talk of the town. People saw me like I was an extra-terrestrial. I was the topic of discussion in the evening tea meetings. Then, one day, soldiers came to my master's house and ordered him to present me before the court the next morning. I was afraid at the mention of a court, and nevertheless, knew the questions that would be put up. As I didn't want to answer any of them, I ran from the house at night. Without bidding a goodbye, or exchanging words of care and affection, I simply left them. I walked out of the whole empire."

"Where did you go then?" Shahista asked.

"I began walking south. I walked for months together, until I was accepted by wanderers. In my solitary journey, I starved for days and got frail, I had to bear many injuries, but they healed before time, I faced chronic diseases, natural disasters, and extreme climatic conditions, but I didn't die. I survived through all of it."

13 - CLASSIFIED TRANSFORMATION

Back in the woods, the man, impatiently checked his digital watch, and knew he had no more time to waste. The plan had to be executed soon. I ought to call him for the last time, he thought, taking his cell phone out of his pocket. He had to confirm the whereabouts of his partner before he decided to storm into the facility alone. His partner rejected the call. He might be close to the target, the man mused. He then decided to drop off a voice note that said, "I am entering the facility as per our plan. You too stick to it."

He then readied himself with heavy arms and ammunitions; his face still hidden behind a black facade, and strode over to the entrance of the facility. Looking around, scanning for the cameras, he found one at the entrance, and watching around for clearance, shot an arrow in its direction. It hit the camera's eye and ruptured it. He then sneaked into the building with his automated arrow shooter, a glass covering one of his eyes, attached with his forehead by a ring that circumvented his head. The glass showed images of men present inside, along with a three dimensional view of the building with all its corridors and rooms, directing him towards the cell where Om had been held captive. He could fix his target with this glass, and then shoot him with his arrows, leaving no room for mistakes. He also had a belt bag tied around his waist with similar sized pockets in the front, the sides, and the rear. There was a metallic piece attached on his right hand from wrist to elbow, with a small arrow placed on its muzzle.

He carried another bag on his back with a PDW 19 assault rifle with a range of 250 ft., 40% stability in its grip, maximum zoom of 20 times, clip size of 25 bullets, which took 4.50 seconds to be reloaded automatically. Two P622 pistols with a range of 150 ft., clip size of 8 bullets that took 3 seconds to reload

After taking a few cautious steps, he saw a guard with a gun in the other corner of the corridor. He slowly moved towards the guard. The glass displayed how far he was from the guard. He then came to a halt and stood still. The glass displayed, "Target reachable!" in a bright green color. It helped to set the hand and eye coordination between the arrow and the target. And, then he shot the first arrow, which hit the target on his head. The guard fell dead instantly. He ran towards the guard, making sure not to make any noise. He checked one of the pockets of his belt bag, took out a fiber plate, set up the time on it, and fixed it on the wall of a hidden corner.

He then moved forward, ready to take the next man down.

On the sea Shore of Ross Island, a chopper landed, followed by a speed boat tearing the sea and reaching the same spot. The man could see the chopper landing slowly. He grabbed his bag and rushed towards it. While sprinting, he loaded his weapons. As men descended from the chopper, they were welcomed with a shower of bullets. Some recoiled back and shot in the man's direction. Veerbhadra got off the chopper and knew that the book he held was The Treasure. So, without wasting any time, he looked around for his jeep, found it, and rushed towards it. The man smelled Veerbhadra's intentions, and to fail them altogether, shot at the wheels of the jeep and then at the driver. Veerbhadra threw himself in the driver's seat as the driver was shot dead instantly and ignited the engine to drive away the punctured jeep to the facility. The other men engaged the shooter, not allowing him to stop Veerbhadra, at the cost of their lives.

Back in the interrogation room, the screen displayed in which Om had a beard, golden earrings, and a tribal crown on his head and was being venerated like god. Om said,

"I didn't know how to cheat, lie or deceive people. I did not take advantage of anybody. Few old men said I was an avatar God had sent for them. They belived serving me was like serving God himself. These people has seen me recover from deadly diseases, walk out of a natural disaster unharmed. This belief continued and my life passed by uneventful for sometime. But then a few young men died out of some unknown disease. People started notcing that I had not aged a day since I joined their clan. All the old men leading the tribe, who believed and worshipped me, died their natural deaths. And with them died their belief. Time changed, their leaders changed, too. I was now looked upon as a curse. A curse, that sucks life out of young people to remain young. They belive I was the reason for the deaths of the young men. A few of them still had good faith in me and fought for me. But the fear of darkness was taking over the light of faith. I was expelled from the tribe. They did not kill me with a fear of a bigger curse.

I was alone again, and now I knew that I had to keep changing my identities and locations. That no one was mentally prepared to accept the truth.

Since then, until now, I have been hiding myself, but..."

The door of the interrogation room opened with a bang and Dr. Srinivasan entered. Om got alarmed. The sudden thrash of the door drew everyone's attention towards Dr. Srinivasan. Furious, Dr Srinivasan saw Om and started walking towards him.

"Sir, are you..." Dr. Batra said, and was interrupted by Dr. Srinivasan, who showed him a palm, a signal to remain quiet.

Dr. Srinivasan grabbed Om's shirt with both his hands, and stared at him with eyes red with anger.

"Sir! What is wrong with you? What are you..." Shahista stood up. Dr. Srinivasan looked into Shahista's eyes, and she instantly knew that not saying anything was the only choice she had right now. Dr. Srinivasan brought his gaze back to Om, only to find him calm and composed as usual, waiting for a question. The old man in the chamber saw all of it and pressed a panic button.

"Evi ayindi Chinna?" Om said.

Dr. Srinivasan calmed down at once listening, *"What happened Chhotu?"* in Om's tone and language. But, the next moment, his fury returned and he replied in Telugu,

"Nenu Chinna kaadu! Naa manasu lo prashanalu unnai, naaku samadhanan kavali."

("I am not Chhotu! I have questions and I want straight answers.")

"Sare, Chinna Kaakpote, em ani pilvali? Kunju?", Om said.
("Okay. If not Chhotu, then what shall I call you? Kunju?")

"Naaku ala yavaru pilavaru, neeku ela telsindi. Nuvuu yavaru?" Dr. Srinivasan replied.
("No one calls me by that name anymore. How can you possibly know that? Who are you?")

Om closed his eyes, and the screen came back to life. The image it projected showed a few students in a classroom, seated on wooden benches of an old shattered government school wearing half pants, white half shirt and slippers. Some of them were barefooted. They were all bullying their classmate, who was sobbing. Then, Om, the teacher, entered the classroom and scolded them all for bullying the kid. He shooed all of them out of the class and sat with the innocent student, started talking to him and calmed him down.

"Neeku adi gurtunda?" Om calmly said.
("Do you remember that?")

Dr. Srinivasan's eyes welled up with tears, and he cried like a kid again. He was compelled to believe in the impossible after seeing his own childhood with Om. He now believed everything Om had said, and saw him with a lot of compassion and respect.

Others present in the room stood clueless as to what was happening there, due to the lack of knowledge of Telegu language and the image whatsoever.

Dr. Shahista came near both of them, just as LSD's computer beeped.

She looked at the screen, which went blank for a second, before the old man's face appeared on it. LSD got alert and pressed enter on the keyboard once. Her screen now displayed a digital watch. 8:43, it read, and the countdown started with each passing second. Her eyes went wide, and she saw Parimal.

He was already looking at her. He had received the same beep and the same face with the same timer. Parimal moved a few steps towards Abhilash's bench, and kept a hand on his shoulder. Suddenly, the jolly and careless hacker changed into a matured and sincere adult. That childish face vanished in the dark. The introvert, silent and scared Parimal suddenly became hyperactive.

As the distance between the jeep and the facility reduced to less than 2 kilometers, the man decided to start running to follow Veerbhadra after he had killed all his men. He now chased him. Veerbhadra, on the other end, reached with the punctured Jeep and entered the building. His body was full of blood spots, even his face was red with blood was smeared over it. He panted heavily as he entered the facility and called Dr. Srinivasan. The armed security guards surrounded him to guard him and were on a high alert.

In the interrogation room, Dr. Srinivasan asked, *"What's in the book?"*

Om smiled with the faith that the books were safe at the place where he had hid them himself. He was unaware of the fact that the books were at the Ross Islannd as him.

"Those books are the answers to the biggest secret in the world, called 'death'. They hold what men have not yet discovered. They contain the key to immortality. They describe the process of making a man similar to me. Time keeps an account of every second in everyone's life. So, you age every day. The books have the ability to make you fall off the vision of the almighty time. Imagine you don't exist for time. For you, death is an illusion. For the one who passes through the book, life will be forever.

No one had yet fathomed the reason behind the sudden change of hearts."

Dr. Srinivasan's phone rang just as he was trying to comprehend what Om had said. It was Veerbhadra. He answered it.

"Sir, I have the book, I am now entering the facility. Someone had followed us to the island. Where are you, sir?" he said, almost out of breath, owing to the rush.

Veerbhadra's voice screeched through the phone so that Om had heard every word of what he had said.

Om's shock was evident on his face and for the first time until now, he felt cheated. All his feeling towards his old student suddenly dried up. He saw Dr. Srinivasan bluntly just as he ordered his man to proceed towards the interrogation room and told him to wait outside until he came and collected the book himself. He hung up the call. His eyes were full of guilt, and his face an epitome of apology. With the same feeling, he said, *"I have committed a mistake, but I never knew I was doing so. I am going to rectify it now. Before I leave, please know that I was not leading this team, someone else was, and it wasn't before today that I knew I stood on the wrong side. All of them are innocent, these kids, they know nothing."*

Om closed his eyes, disappointed, and said, *"What have you done? Whom are you all working for?"*

"I thought I was working for money, so I never tried to know the details of the work. All of them thought they were working for me, and because they trusted my judgment, they asked nothing. I have to leave now, to safeguard the books from filthy hands. I have committed an unpardonable mistake, but please try to forgive me if I fail in my quest", said Dr. Srinivasan, his head bowed out of guilt and shame. Suddenly Dr Srinivasan turned and went near the camera installed on one of the walls for the old man to see

and hit it many times till it did not break in pieces. The old man watched Dr Srinivasan hitting the camera and then the screen went blank. The old man smiled.

Dr. Srinivasan held Om's hands, pressed them into his once, and turned to leave. Om asked *"who paid you to do this?"*

"His name is Nagendra, that is all I know." came the answer while Dr Sriniwasan leaving the room in rush. Om's face turned pale hearing the name. He was as astouned as everyone else listening his story of immortality.

As Dr Srinivasan left Parimal started walking towards the exit.

"Parimal?" Dr. Batra called after him.

"Going for a smoke" said Parimal without looking behind.

Dr. Batra and Shahista looked at each other surprisingly as this time Parimal did not stammer. While LSD kept herself engrossed in pressing the keys on her computer, she really looked as if in a haste.

As Parimal got away from the sight of the team mates, he ran as fast as he could towards the kitchen which was right behind the facility after three right turns from the door at the end of the corridors. He reached the kitchen, went to the common wall between the kitchen and the facility and stood there waiting for something impatiently. He checked his watch every now and then. The old man still sat behind his desk, noticing every move of everyone.

Dr. Batra and Dr. Shahista stood stunned in the middle of the room looking at the change in the atmosphere around them. They were witnessing Dr. Srinivasan conversing with Om Shastri with a lot of gratitude and respect, his eyes all in tears. His body language revealed that like LSD and Parimal, he too was in a hurry. Abhilash lay down in his chair sleeping with his head on the desk.

LSD was totally into her computer, and now was typing a code which was tattooed on her left toe. *"1 Corinthians 15:51"*, read the code.

It meant, "Victory over death".

As she pressed enter on the keyboard, the wall where Parimal was waiting, transformed into a door. A few bricks fell off and a small screen with a touch keypad asked for a code. He typed in the same code, "1 Corinthians 15:51" The door opened. It was a narrow passage between the walls, only 3 feet wide, and 16 feet long. A narrow hidden room came into view that had never existed before today. A room full of all kinds of weapons used for assassination, bulletproof armors and suits. This passage had white light with every weapon placed on the walls. It had another door opposite the first one. This door opened back into the interrogation room. Parimal started picking things up without wasting any time.

LSD was continuously eyeing everyone to find a moment of solitary. She now had it. She rushed towards the wash-rooms at the corner of the interrogation room.

The masked man had brutally killed guards in the corridor, without any noise whatsoever. Then his partner entered the facility, and openly shot everyone he saw dressed in a uniform. The gunshots echoed in the facility, and deafened everyone inside it. As all the guards rushed to the entrance, the first partner's path cleared up and saved him a lot of time in reaching the interrogation room.

Om heard the gunshot along with Shahista and Dr. Batra. He at once came into action and requested them to free him or there might be grave consequences which they would not live to see.

Abhilash didn't react and kept his slumber alive. Dr. Batra approached him and Shahista went to Om, fighting in her head the dilemma of right and wrong. Dr. Batra tried to jolt Abhilash awake, but he lay there all the same. Dr. Batra checked his pulse, only to find him dead. Shahista panicked, and decided to untie Om. Parimal had killed Abhilash the moment he had seen the old man's face on the computer. How and why were question that nobody in the interrogation room had the answer to.

Dr. Srinivasan reached the corridor of the chamber and told Veerbhadra to hand him over the book. Veerbhadra, unaware of the gravity of the situation, handed over the book to him. Dr. Srinivasan hugged the book tight on his chest, and started back towards the interrogation room. The old man saw it all. He picked up an earpiece and pressed a button.

"Lizz...?" he whispered in his throaty voice.

LSD inside the wash room listened intently from a similar kind of an earpiece, and replied, *"Yes, sir."* She stood on a tap and pulled an unseen and unapproachable bag kept on the loft of the washroom.

Then Parimal who had gone inside the passage, and the one who came out of it, were two entirely different men, and yet were the same.

In the interrogation room, as Dr. Batra and Shahista struggled to untie Om, LSD came out. Shahista and Dr. Batra witness a severe transformation in her. They saw her walking towards them with a pair of automated P6 22 pistols with 150 feet of range and 8 bullets clip sized which took 3 seconds to reload.

The same pistols as the man who was now approaching the interrogation room had tied to his thighs.

This man's partner, heavily loaded with artilleries, blasted the front entrance with a bazooka, with many casualties in a single shot. It was impossible for the guards to locate the man in the thick woods. The sun was going down with each passing moment.

In the facility, as Dr. Srinivasan entered the interrogation room, he saw LSD, and instantly knew that not all the members were as innocent as he had imagined.

He was panting heavily as he stepped into the room. He tried to pretend that nothing had happened, but LSD had decided his fate. As Dr. Srinivasan read LSD's eyes, she smiled sarcastically. All was quiet before LSD coldly shot Dr. Srinivasan in the chest, and snatched the book from him.

Dr. Srinivasan fell on the floor and blood rinsed out from his body. He died slowly, feeling all the pain he was meant to. Dr. Batra and Shahista stood in utter shock, watching Dr. Srinivasan breathing his last, and LSD brutally behaving. Guilt was far from her. The old man back in the chamber smiled, as he saw the book in LSD's hands. LSD aimed at Dr. Batra and Shahista together, and warned, *"Don't! Or before you will even realise that I have a knack of using both my hands simultaneously, your souls will have met their maker"*.

Om witnessed everything in the process of being untied.

"You want to kill us? You will really shoot at us, huh?" Shahista said in a rather courageous tone.

"If the need be", came the blunt reply from LSD.

"What are you waiting for, then?" Shahista questioned.

LSD smiled a shameless one, and said, *"My orders"*, walking towards the only exit of the room, and locking it from the inside.

After ending the lives of two more guards who stood right outside the doors of the interrogation room, in the way which was his liking of assassination, in peace and in quiet, the man parted with his mask, and his glasses, too. He had long white hair, and well built body. He took off the armour from his chest, and had on big golden wrist rings encircling both his wrists. He picked up his bow and arrow with his left hand and kicked the door of the interrogation room hard.

Parimal, loaded with the ammunitions, reached the old man's room, and sat on the floor at his knees. The old man pampered him. While he pampered Parimal, the old man kept an eye on all the visuals on the screen. Suddenly, he saw someone killing the men on the door of the interrogation room, and trying to break it open. He pointed towards the screen in order to show it to Parimal.

At once, the Parimal sitting calmly, got ferocious. He stood up in one fine movement and went for Om Shastri and LSD.

14 - DEATHLESS WARRIORS

The other partner had nearly cleared the front gate, when only Veerbhadra and two of his men remained to be conquered. Dr. Shahista showed some courage and started untying Om again.

Sensing that, the old man ordered LSD to kill both of them, and bring Om to him, alive.

LSD sarcastically smiled again, and then aimed at Dr. Shahista and Dr. Batra with both her hands, and shot simultanoeusly. Dr. Batra voluntarily gave way to the bullet owing to his faster reflexes. But, the second bullet had hit its target well. Only not for whom it was intended. Dr. Shahista had her eyes on Om, Om's set upon LSD, and LSD's on Shahista. So, Om had a moment to react before she shot Shahista. Om had replaced himself with Shahista unintentionally in a trial to save the selfless savior. The bullet hit Om's back. Both Shahista and Om fell on the ground at a distance from each other. LSD realized that she had committed a huge mistake by shooting at Om. Without thinking about it, she aimed at Shahista once again. Om lay on the floor watching it helplessly, wincing in pain. After a moment, Dr. Shahista was shot in her chest.

Parimal entered the passage room, passing through the kitchen to reach directly to the interrogation room through the hidden passage. On the other side, the main door to the interrogation room was too weak to bear another kick now. LSD held Om by his collars and dragged him towards a wall, looking around for Dr. Batra at the same time. Out in the corridor, Veerbhadra fell back slowly hitting the kitchen door as the man entered the building. Parimal entered the password to unlock the door to enter the interrogation room. A few bricks fell inside the interrogation room where LSD waited for Parimal to arrive and Om Shastri bled heavily. The man goes for the final kick just then, and the door comes apart. Everyone in the room stood stupefied as they comprehended the face that entered in. The face was one of the images that had an imprint in Om's memory and thereby had appeared on the screen. He was the man Om had claimed to be searching for a thousand years. He was an epitome of the past standing abreast with the present, fully equipped to look time in its eyes.

He was Parshuram!

His face had on it the same rage and fury of Lord Shiva. He had big eyes that hid nothing, and strong hands capable of lifting a mountain.

From the other end, walked in the other partner, another person back from death, Ashwathama, as they all knew him. Veerbhadra saw him and immediately knew that he had seen him in Om's memories of Ashwathama and Subhash Chandra Bose. Veerbhadra, terrified, ran towards the chamber of the old man.

Parshuram saw Om, bleeding, and hostage, in the hands of LSD, and his eyes burnt with rage. He lifted his bow to shoot at her, just when the bricks fell and the door opened. Behind LSD, Parimal walked in, ready to attack Parshurama. He rushed to get in the front of LSD, took an aim, and shot at Parshuram before he could have shot LSD. Parshurama missed the target as he defended himself from Parimal. Meanwhile, LSD entered the passage room and dragged Om along with her. Om felt an immense pain and found it impossible to stand. Dr. Batra saw it all as he hid behind a stainless steel operating table. Both Parshuram and Parimal shot at each other, but in the ambush, Parimal had managed to rescue LSD and Om. He ordered LSD to press the button that closed the door which could then not be opened from outside. LSD pushed the button, and Parimal ran towards it to make it to the door. Parshuram knew that this was the last shot he could take at Parimal, so he lifted his farsaa (axe) and threw it on the door, screaming, and wild in anger. The aim was perfect, the strength with which the weapon was thrown, was enough to cut Parimal into two halves, but before it could hit him, the doors slid close, catching the weapon in line with the slit of the opening.

Parshuram ran towards the door, but knew that it was late. As Parmial crossed the hidden passage, being followed by LSD who still dragged Om, they had reached the kitchen, and kept walking towards the corridor that followed, to advance to the old man's chamber. They saw Veerbhadra coming towards the kitchen's corridor, heading to the same place where they intended to reach. Veerbhadra saw them too, rushing out of the kitchen, with all their arms and ammunitions. He followed their gaze, to see that Om bled, and marked their trail with the blood gushing out of him. Veerbhadra stood stupefied at the scenario. Something inside him compelled him to take aim at Parimal, a gut instinct it was. And, he had learnt from his experience that gut instincts are to be followed, always! So he grabbed his gun and aimed it at Parimal.

"What are you doing? Who the hell are you?" he thundered. His voice echoed in the glass corridor for some seconds before fading away.

Parimal replied to this by aiming his weapon towards Veerbhadra, too. LSD gestured Parimal to put down his gun, but Parmial refused to agree. LSD then lowered his gun with her hand, slowly.

"Veerbhadra, we are a part of your team. We are taking him to Nagendra sir. Please come along."

"How did he get injured and who is Nagendra sir?" Veerbhadra asked, raising an eyebrow.

"A man attacked us all inside the interrogation room, and tried to kill him. We somehow managed to save him. There is no time to explain the rest. We should first reach at a safe spot before sorting things out between us. For now just know that we are on the same team. Believe me.", LSD replied rather concealing her expressions at the lie.

Om heard every word LSD said, but he did not counter her. He was in too much pain to talk and also because he knew that on knowing the truth, Veerbhadra would attack them. Om also knew that Veerbhadra stood no chance of winning in front of these two skilled fighters. So, he decided to remain silent for the moment.

Veerbhadra nodded at the theory served to him, and accompanied them to the chamber. Veerbhadra now held Om and assisted him in walking. The time lost in talking with Veerbhadra had lessened the distance between them and Ashwatthama, who was now just a turn behind them. Parshuram, who had to cover the longer corridor from the interrogation room to the kitchen which was exactly behind the interrogation room, and three right turns away was on his run.

In the chamber, the old man looked at the screen for the last time to calculate how much time they would all take to bring Om in there. Then, he powered down the screen, and decided they were 3 minutes down. He then moved the screen sideways to reveal a lock code pattern affixed on the wall behind it. He then pressed a few buttons on the keypad of the lock screen.

Suddenly, a few cracks surfaced on three of the walls, excluding the ones containing the entrance door and the exit door. He then pressed a few more keys, and the cracks emerged as numerous doors on all sides, opening in different directions, and into long dark passages. As the walls parted and the doors appeared, one of the marble tiles on the floor-8 feet by 5 feet in size- descended below its level, and moved horizontally under its adjacent tile, to bring to the fore, a staircase that was hidden beneath the floor. The old man had safely wrapped both the books in a blood red cloth, which he now hid inside a bag, along with some medicines and a few other books. Now, he waited for Parimal and LSD to arrive, and hid the keypad behind the screen again.

Parimal and LSD had almost reached the door to the old man's chamber, which was being guarded by two guards. Veerbhadra was close behind their heels, as had to carry Om's weight added to his own, which slowed him down. But, there was nothing that slowed down Ashwatthama and Parshuram in catching their hold. Just when Parimal entered the code to open the door, Ashwatthama took the last turn, and now could see them. The opponents stood at the two corners of the long corridor, barely 20 feet apart, closest to Ashwatthama stood Veerbhadra.

Ashwatthama aimed at Veerbhadra, who held Om and started walking towards Parimal and LSD, cautiously. Veerbhadra, LSD, and Parimal stood clueless, their backs towards Ashwatthama. But, the security guards saw him, and began shooting ferociously at once. Veerbhadra, LSD, and Parimal got alarmed and realized how near the danger had been lurking. Ashwatthama's target had shifted to the guards now. As he shot one of them in the head, a bullet from behind him, cleared through the other's chest. He turned around to find Parshuram, dropping his hands after the successful shot.

Meanwhile, Parimal and LSD entered the chamber and began a series of attacks on their foes, from the inside. Veerbhadra, under the impression that he fought for the righteous, laid Om down against the wall, and bravely fought to save Om and other team members.

Back in the interrogation room, Dr. Batra stood near Abhilash, who had been deceptively killed by Parimal back then, and then approached Dr. Shahista, and cried bitterly, at the loss he was witnessing.

But, his grievances faded as he realised that his own life was at stake, too. That he was still alive, but he knew not till when. The gunshots in the distance broke his reverie. He had to devise a plan to escape from the building from the other side. He gathered evidences and samples of Om's blood, LSD's laptop, and Om's file which contained all the pictures, and names he had been using all the way and sneaked out of the building.

Veerbhadra fought like a real soldier before being shot first by Parshuram on his shoulder, and then by Ashwatthama in his chest and stomach. He fell into Om's lap, looked above at his face, and apologized for failing to save him. Om's eyes filled with tears as Veerbhadra breathed his last in his arms.

LSD screamed from inside the chamber, and banged her fists on the door that separated her from Om and Veerbhadra. She looked at Veerbhadra and desired to see him for the last time, but Parimal held her back, since he knew that the enemies weren't far away. Om saw towards L.S.D's scream and saw the Old man standing with Parimal and L.S.D with his blur vision. He could recognize Nagendra partially.Parimal closed another door, with a heavy heart. Ashwatthama rushed towards Om to ensure he was fine, and Parshuram rushed towards the closing door of the chamber.

"Guruji, he is bleeding profusely!" Ashwatthama exclaimed.

Parshuram was busy fixing detonators on the door, and replied, *"Tear his shirt, and tie it to his wounds tightly. He can't die, but he mustn't faint as well. Take him away from this door, and stay with him all the time. I am going after them".*

"As you order Guruji."

Ashwatthama took Om back to the kitchen and started searching for the first-aid kit while Om laid comfortably in one of the working tables.

Om looked at Parshuram and the door, one after another, and then found himself at a loss for words.

He had so many questions, but was slowly losing his consciousness.

"I have been searching you since Yugas. I knew you were there", he managed to speak.

"You were always on our radar. We never lost your track. You never found us because we didn't want you to", Ashwatthama revealed.

"How did you find me here?"

"We tracked down a few men from your locker in one of the banks down here to Ross Island."

Om was taken aback on hearing this. The truth then dawned upon him that people had been to the Srilankan caves while he was detained at this place. Upset, he asked, *"Where are the books?"*

Ashwatthama's face grew grim.

"They are with them, in their possession. Guruji has gone after them for the same cause", Ashwatthama said in a disappointed tone.

"Why have you come for me? Why are you saving me?" Om asked.

"Because, you hold the key to the end."

Om, surprised, looked at him, and fought the heaviness that weighed on his mind. Gradually, he let his mind drift into the darkness, and fell on the table in front of him.

Parshuram blasted the steel door and entered the old man's chamber. He saw numerous doors then, and faced the dilemma of which one to choose in order to follow his enemies.

As LSD and Parimal had entered the chamber, they, along with their boss, had hidden under the tile which opened up a staircase. The tile had been shut properly again. Now, as Parshuram looked around, he saw nothing out of ordinary. He randomly chose a door, and opened it. A long corridor unveiled itself. Parshuram started sprinting inside it. But, to his dismay, he soon met a dead end at the other corner. He tried another one, but all in vain. Then, he gave up. The other bombs he had affixed in different corners of the facility would blow any time now, of which, Om and Ashwatthama were unaware. So, he rushed back towards the kitchen. There, he found Ashwatthama removing the bullet from Om's body.

LSD, Parimal, and the old man hadn't waited there at all. The passage was a secret one, skillfully built. It opened up to the sea shore.

The three came under the sky, on the sandy terrain. A submarine had already been waiting for them. They ascended it, and left the island with the books.

Parshuram, along with Ashwatthama had just come out of the building when it blew off. The facility, so artistically made, reduced to nothing within a few minutes.

Their enemies too saw this phenomenon, though from a different corner of the island.

"Where are the books?" Ashwatthama asked.

"They are with them", Parshuram replied.

"And where are they?"

"They have left the island"

"But, they have the books. What will our next move be?"

"Our next move is to keep Om safe. It's time for him to know who he was before being Mrityunjay. Remind him of his truth. We will need the actual him the next time we face them."

"But, how will we find them now? We have no clue where they might have gone!" Ashwatthama grew more and more anxious.

"They will come for us. We don't have to go searching for them."

"Why will they come for us? They already have what they want."

"They will soon realize that we hold the final key to the lock of immortality", said Parshuram looking in Om's direction.

"They will need a drip of Om's blood to complete the procedure of immortality for which they will have to come searching for us again."

Secreted on another corner of the island, frightened to death was Dr Batra, with the blood sample that Parshuram thought only they have in form of Om.

"Guruji, what do we do now?"

"We only wait", assured Parshuram.

By the dawn, they stood near the sea above the rocks, waiting for another wave to hit it, as one which had just passed, had failed to break it.

Parshuram stood firm at the edge of the rock, taking in the beauty of the sun, setting in the horizon. Ashwatthama asked Om *"Do you have any idea who they were?"*

"Nagendra." Om replied.

"How is it possible? Nagendra is long lost" asked Ashwatthama.

Parshuram answered still looking at the setting sun." *Long lost.........not dead. Just lost"*

Nagendra impatiently started reading the book, with eyes gleaming like that of a child's at the sight of his favourite candy as Parimal drove the U-boat far from the island. LSD looked at nothing. Far away, in the sky, the sun was setting taking away with it the bright blue sky, leaving behind...............a darkness.

To be continued......................

Printed in the United States
By Bookmasters